He wanted to r

Sweat beaded on his brow, and he silently ca——

He couldn't do any of those things because as hard as he'd tried not to care about her, he was starting to have feelings for her.

She looked up at him with that sweet, seductive look as they walked into her den, and he gruffly ordered her to go to bed and get some sleep.

Hurt flickered in her eyes, but he assured himself it was for the best. She didn't argue. She hurried to her bedroom, making him feel like a heel.

Exhaustion tugged at his limbs, and even though he didn't think he could sleep, he stretched out on Megan's sofa. He laid his gun by his side just in case of trouble, then closed his eyes.

He could practically hear her whisper his name as if she wanted him to come to her.

Furious with himself, he rolled to his side to face the door, a reminder of the reason he couldn't leave. Megan was in danger, and he wouldn't let anything happen to her.

If anyone tried, they'd have to kill him first.

WARRIOR SON

USA TODAY Bestselling Author
RITA HERRON

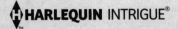

HARLEQUIN INTRIGUE®

For Sue, a cowboy lover!

Recycling programs
for this product may
not exist in your area.

ISBN-13: 978-0-373-74962-1

Warrior Son

Copyright © 2016 by Rita B. Herron

Printed in U.S.A.

USA TODAY bestselling author **Rita Herron** wrote her first book when she was twelve but didn't think real people grew up to be writers. Now she writes so she doesn't have to get a real job. A former kindergarten teacher and workshop leader, she traded storytelling to kids for writing romance, and now she writes romantic comedies and romantic suspense. Rita lives in Georgia with her family. She loves to hear from readers, so please visit her website, ritaherron.com.

Books by Rita Herron

The Heroes of Horseshoe Creek

Lock, Stock and McCullen
McCullen's Secret Son
Roping Ray McCullen
Warrior Son

Bucking Bronc Lodge

Certified Cowboy
Cowboy in the Extreme
Cowboy to the Max
Cowboy Cop
Native Cowboy
Ultimate Cowboy

Harlequin Intrigue

Cold Case at Camden Crossing
Cold Case at Carlton's Canyon
Cold Case at Cobra Creek
Cold Case in Cherokee Crossing

Visit the Author Profile page at Harlequin.com for more titles.

CAST OF CHARACTERS

Deputy Roan Whitefeather—He's determined to get justice for the McCullens, but no one can know that he's also Joe's son.

Dr. Megan Lail—The ME discovered that Joe McCullen didn't die of natural causes. Will her pursuit of the truth get her killed?

Joe McCullen—The patriarch of the family has secrets that keep haunting from the grave.

Grace McCullen—She died in a car accident when her sons were small. But was it really an accident, or did someone want her dead?

Dr. Cumberland—The McCullens' doctor and family friend is shocked to learn Joe was murdered. How did he miss the signs that his friend was poisoned?

Barbara Lowman—Joe's mistress resented him for not marrying her. Did she kill his wife so she could have Joe to herself?

Bobby Lowman—Did he kill his father because he didn't make him a McCullen?

Dale Hummings—He blames Megan for his brother's incarceration. Is he trying to kill her out of revenge?

Morty and Edith Bennett—Were they killed because they knew the name of the person who murdered Joe?

Arlis Bennett and Boyle Gates—Roan believes these cousins are behind the sabotage at Horseshoe Creek. Would either have had Joe killed to force his sons to sell Horseshoe Creek?

Bart Dunn—He and his wife lost a baby years ago. Does he know something about Joe McCullen's murder?

Chapter One

Deputy Roan Whitefeather didn't belong on Mc-Cullen land.

Yet here he stood at the edge of the party celebrating Ray McCullen's marriage to Scarlet Lovett like the outsider he was.

Even though he was blood related to the McMullen men. Even though Joe McCullen was also his father.

He was alone. And he would keep it that way.

Maddox, Brett and Ray had no idea that he was their half brother. Hell, he hadn't known until a few months ago when his mother died and he'd found that damn birth certificate.

And after the trouble the McCullens had this past week—two fires on the ranch—and the bombshell that Joe had a son named Bobby with his mistress, Barbara, Roan would keep the truth about his paternity quiet.

A noise sounded from the hill to the right, and he pivoted, senses honed. Since they still hadn't apprehended the person responsible for the fires, he had to keep an eye out for trouble. With the entire family in celebratory mode, their guards were down. Which would give anyone with a grudge against the McCullens the perfect opportunity to attack.

Maddox, the town sheriff and Roan's boss, stepped in front of the group gathered on the lawn by the creek and raised his champagne glass to toast the happy couple.

For a moment envy mushroomed inside him as he watched Ray kiss Scarlet, and the other brothers and their wives congratulating and hugging one another.

They had weathered some storms, but they were one big happy family now.

The only family he'd ever known was his mother and the people on the res.

He didn't need family or anyone else, he reminded himself.

Still, he'd protect the McCullens because it was his job. And his job was all that mattered to him.

Although questions nagged at him. If Joe McCullen had known about Roan, would he have spent time with him? Would he have brought him to Horseshoe Creek and introduced him to his half brothers?

Or would he have hidden him away like he had his other illegitimate son Bobby Lowman?

The wind blew the trees rustling the leaves, and he scanned the horizon again. The ranch spread for hundreds of miles, livestock and horses roaming the pastures. Joe McCullen had definitely built a legacy here for his sons. And although Ray and Brett had been gone for years, they'd recently returned and planned to help Maddox run the ranch.

Someone didn't want the McCullens to thrive, though. Someone who might have a grudge against Joe besides his mistress and son, Bobby. For all he knew, the problems could be about the land or the way Joe did business.

Hell, if Maddox, Brett or Ray knew Roan was blood related, they might accuse *him* of sabotage.

All the more reason to keep quiet about who he was.

And all the more reason to keep his questions about Joe's death to himself until he found out if there was any substance to his suspicions.

DR. MEGAN LAIL finished her autopsy report on a man named Morty Burns, a ranch hand who'd been shot and left dead outside Pistol Whip, Wyoming. So far, the police had no idea who'd shot him, but she'd done her job—established time and cause of death and recovered the bullet that had taken the man's life.

She had been infatuated with dead bodies since her sister's murder. Not that she enjoyed the morbid side of death, but the bodies told the story.

Just as she'd been driven to know who killed Shelly, family members deserved to know the answers about their loved ones. And it was comforting to know she could help give them closure.

Still, her father had been disappointed in her. He'd raved about Shelly and her beauty, constantly reminding Megan that she hadn't been graced with extraordinary looks, that she had to use her brain to get anywhere in life. She hadn't minded that at all. Science had always interested her.

When Shelly had been killed and investigators had converged, she'd realized that the medical examiner was the one who'd discovered the clue that led to the culprit. Sitting at the trial with her father, she'd decided she wanted to be an ME.

She removed her gloves, filed her report, then clicked to the news and studied the story about the recent arrest of Bobby and Barbara Lowman made by Deputy Roan Whitefeather and the sheriff. The arrests had hit big in Pistol Whip because they centered around the McCullens of Horseshoe Creek and revealed that the patriarch of the family, Joe, who had recently died, had another family on the side.

A mistress named Barbara and an illegitimate son, Bobby.

Bobby had resented Joe for years, and his mother Barbara felt betrayed because Joe never married her. They'd also been upset over the stipulations Joe placed on the will regarding Bobby's inheritance, that Bobby would have to work under the tutelage of Maddox.

They'd pulled a gun on Scarlet and threatened the family, and both were in prison. But neither admitted to setting the two fires on the ranch, one of which had ruined the family's long-standing home.

More details followed in the article.

Former rodeo star Brett McCullen has offered a $10,000 reward for information leading to the arrest of the arsonist.

Megan massaged her temple as her mind took a leap. Something had been bothering her about Joe McCullen's autopsy.

Her curious nature, the attribute that helped her most in her job, pummeled her with what-ifs. What if Joe's death hadn't been due to his illness?

She'd detected something odd about the tox screen and relayed her concerns to Dr. Cumberland, the McCullens' family doctor and Joe's lifelong friend.

The conversation replayed in her head.

"You're young and new to this, Megan. You obviously made a mistake," Dr. Cumberland had said. "I took care of Joe during his illness. He had emphysema. Just look at his X-rays and scans."

She'd looked at them and Joe had in fact had emphysema. "But there are slight traces of a toxin indicating he was poisoned. It appears to be cyanide."

Dr. Cumberland had scanned her notes and scowled. "Run the tests again. This can't be right."

Megan had gone to the lab, extracted another sample and sent it to be tested. An hour later, Dr. Cumberland had hand delivered the report to her.

"See, there is no sign of poison. The lab tech mixed up the reports. The result you first received was for another case."

Yet the fact that someone was trying to hurt the McCullens bothered her. She was meticulous in her work and never made mistakes.

And she couldn't let this go without one more look. Adrenaline pumping, she accessed the autopsy file. Guilt nagged at her for questioning Dr. Cumberland, though.

The family physician had worked in Pistol Whip for years. Everyone in town adored him. For goodness' sake, he'd delivered half the town's babies, including the McCullen boys, Maddox, Brett and Ray.

And he had been distraught over Joe's death.

He wouldn't have had any reason to lie to her or cover up a tox report.

But…something just didn't feel right. She didn't think she'd made a mistake…

She picked up the phone and called the lab tech, a young guy named Howard, then explained about the two different results.

"I guess it's possible that I mixed them up," Howard said. "But I double-check everything. I'm OCD that way."

So was she. In their line of work, details were important.

Howard cleared his throat. "If you still have a sample I can retest."

Megan's pulse hammered. "As a matter of fact, I do. I'll send it over right now, Howard. But please keep this between you and me."

"Sure, Megan. What's going on?"

"I just want to double-check for myself."

He agreed to call her when he was done, and she decided she'd talk to Deputy Whitefeather while she waited on the results. He would know if Joe had any enemies.

She didn't want to bother Joe's sons unless she had something concrete.

The thought of seeing the deputy again stirred a hot sensation deep in her belly. She'd met Roan when he worked on the res on the tribal council.

When his mother died, she'd performed the autopsy. Roan had been devastated. His mother was all the family he had.

She'd hated to see the big, strong man in pain. A comforting hug had led to a kiss. A kiss filled with such loneliness that she hadn't been able to resist. They'd made love for hours.

Sometimes at night when she was alone, she closed her eyes and could still feel his big, strong hands touching her, stroking her, loving her. She'd never felt anything so intense.

But the next morning, he'd walked away from her and hadn't spoken to her since.

What would he say if she showed up with questions about Joe McCullen's death?

Roan congratulated the happy couple before he drove back to the cabin he'd rented on the river. He missed the res, but working for the sheriff's department meant he worked for all the people in Pistol Whip and the county it encompassed, so living in a neutral, more central location seemed wisest.

"Did you see anything suspicious tonight?" Maddox asked as they watched Scarlet toss the bouquet.

"No. I'll ride across the property on my way home and take a look around, though."

"Thanks." Maddox shook his hand. "I appreciate you covering the office while Rose and I were gone. Brett said he was going to hire extra security for the ranch for a while, at least until we find out who set those fires. He's rebuilding the barns and the main house is already done."

"Extra security is not a bad idea," Roan said. Maddox, Brett and Ray couldn't keep up the ranch and do surveillance around the clock by themselves.

After all, on a spread this size, there were dozens of places for someone to hide.

Some blonde caught the bouquet, prompting squeals from the guests, and Maddox joined his wife on the dance floor.

Roan leaned against the edge of the makeshift bar they'd set up for the reception, his mouth watering for a cold beer. But he didn't drink on the job.

The McCullen men danced and swayed with their wives, and for some odd reason, a pang hit him. They looked so damn happy.

They were family.

Something he didn't have anymore.

Yet…they were his blood kin.

It doesn't matter. You're not going to tell them.

Hell, they'd probably think he was like Bobby Lowman, that he wanted something from them.

He wanted nothing but to live in peace. Caring about folks meant pain when they went away.

His mother's face flashed in his mind. Truth be known, she was the only person in the world he'd ever loved.

His phone buzzed, and he checked the number, surprised to see Dr. Megan Lail's name appear. Damn, he hadn't seen her since last year, the night his mother died.

Since the night they'd…gotten hot and sweaty between the sheets.

Perspiration broke out on his brow and he swiped at it. It was the most erotic sex he'd ever had. For months he'd dreamed about it, woken up to an image of Megan's breasts swaying above him as she impaled herself on his shaft. Of him pumping inside her, of her ivory skin blushing with passion and her soft moans of ecstasy filling the air.

The phone jarred him again, and he cursed and stepped aside, away from the festivities so he could hear. She was the ME, after all. She might have news about a case.

"Deputy Whitefeather."

"Roan, it's Dr. Lail. Megan."

The sound of her husky voice triggered more memories of their lovemaking and made his body go rock hard.

He kept his reply short, afraid he'd give away the yearning in his voice if he said too much. "Yeah?"

"I need to see you."

His breath stalled in his chest. She *needed* him? Instantly his thoughts turned to worry. What if the damn condoms hadn't worked that night? They'd made love—how many times?

"Megan, what's wrong? Are you okay?"

"I'm fine," she said softly, arousing tender feelings inside him. Feelings he didn't want to have.

"Then why did you call?"

Her sharp intake indicated he'd been brusque.

"I'm sorry, if this is a bad time, I can call back."

Now he *had* to know the reason for her call. "No, it's fine. I'm standing guard at Ray McCullen's wedding in case that arsonist strikes again."

"That's sort of the reason I called."

He frowned, his gaze piercing the night as he pivoted to scan the pastures. "Do you have information that could help?"

"I'm not sure," she said. "But I had some questions about Joe McCullen's autopsy."

Roan went completely still. "What kind of questions?"

"I don't feel comfortable discussing it over the phone. Can we meet?"

An image of her unruly, long wavy hair surfaced.

Although she usually wore it in a tight bun, the moment he'd yanked that bun free, he'd unleashed some kind of sexual animal that she kept hidden from the world.

Seeing her was not a good idea.

"Please," she said. "It's important. And…you're the only one I trust."

Damn, did she have to put it that way?

"All right. Where are you?"

"I'm still at the morgue. But I'd prefer to meet you somewhere else."

He could go to her place. But that would be too personal. Too tempting.

"I'll be done soon. How about we meet at The Silver Bullet in an hour?"

She agreed and hung up. For the next hour, Roan watched the celebration wind down. The happy couple kissed and said goodbye as they rushed to the limo Ray had rented. They were headed to the airport to fly to Mexico for their honeymoon.

He left the security team Brett had hired to watch over the ranch, took a quick drive across the property, looking for any stray vehicle or a fire, but all seemed quiet.

By the time he reached The Silver Bullet, he was sweating just thinking about seeing Megan again. He spotted her in a booth to the side when he entered. Country music blared from the speakers, smoke clogged the room and footsteps pounded from the line dance on the dance floor.

Megan looked up at him, one hand clenching a wineglass, her eyes worried. He ordered a beer and joined her. She'd secured her hair in that bun again, she wore no makeup and her clothes were nondescript. Once again it struck him that she downplayed her looks. He wondered why.

She could wear a damn feed sack and she'd still be the prettiest girl he'd ever met. And he knew what she looked like with that hair down, her body naked, her lips trailing kisses down his chest.

"Megan," he said as he slipped into the booth across from her.

"Thank you for coming." She licked her lips, drawing his eyes to her mouth. He took a sip of beer to stall and wrangle his libido.

"You said it was important." *Please spit it out so I can go home and forget about you.*

Not that he ever had. But he was trying.

"Roan, I may be jumping the gun, but I had to talk to someone about this."

The worry in her voice sounded serious. He straightened. "What is it?"

She looked down in her glass. "When I performed Joe McCullen's autopsy the first time, I…thought I saw something suspicious in his tox report."

Roan's heart jumped.

"With all that's happened at Horseshoe Creek recently," Megan continued, "and with that Lowman woman and her son, and those fires…it made me think of that report."

"I don't understand," Roan said. "What was it that bothered you?"

She inhaled a deep breath, then glanced around the room warily, as if she didn't want anyone to hear their conversation. His instincts roared to life. She'd said she didn't feel comfortable talking on the phone.

"Megan, tell me," he said.

"I don't think Joe McCullen died of natural causes." She leaned closer, her voice low. "I think he was murdered."

Chapter Two

Megan's words reverberated in Roan's ears. *Joe McCullen was murdered.*

"How?"

"Poison. Cyanide."

"Are you sure?"

Megan winced. "Not exactly, but—"

"But what?" He leaned across the table, speaking in a hushed tone. "Why did you come to me if you don't know?"

She fiddled with a strand of hair, tucking it back in that bun. He wanted to unknot it and run his fingers through it.

But he had to focus.

"I know what I saw in that initial report. But Dr. Cumberland made me question my results and ran it again. That's when it came back normal."

"So you have one bad test and one normal one?"

"Yes."

"Go on."

She fidgeted with her little round glasses, pushing them up on her nose. "I talked to the lab tech and he's meticulous with details. He didn't think he mixed up the reports like Dr. Cumberland said."

"Everyone makes mistakes," Roan said.

"I know." Megan took a sip of her wine. "But I've seen this guy's work. He's OCD. He checks things at least three times."

Roan didn't know how to respond.

If Megan was right, that meant Joe had been murdered.

But they couldn't make accusations without something more concrete. That would only cause more trouble for the McCullens.

If she was right, though, then someone had gotten away with killing Joe—his father. And he couldn't let that happen.

"Anyway, I talked to the lab tech," Megan said. "I preserved a sample and he's going to retest it."

Roan gave a clipped nod. "When will you have the results?"

"Probably tomorrow. I asked him to keep it quiet."

"Good." His gaze met hers. "Don't tell anyone else about this, Megan. You don't want to create panic if there's nothing to it."

A wary look flashed in those dark brown eyes. "Of course I won't say anything. But if it's true, someone needs to find out who poisoned Joe McCullen."

"And how they did it," Roan muttered. "It would have been difficult with Dr. Cumberland monitoring his health." And there was no way he could accuse the good doctor of foul play. Roan knew Cumberland personally. He was the most compassionate man Roan had ever met. He'd donated time to the res when they needed a Western doctor.

He'd even treated Roan's mother. For God's sake, he'd held her hand and comforted her before she passed.

But Joe could have had visitors. Someone could have slipped something to him when nobody was watching.

"What if Barbara or her son, Bobby, did it?" Megan said. "You know Barbara got tired of waiting on Joe to marry her. Maybe she decided to kill him and get what was owed her."

Roan frowned. "True. But if he was sick anyway, why kill him? Why not wait until the disease got the best of him?"

MEGAN CONSIDERED ROAN'S STATEMENT. Why *would* someone go to the trouble to kill a man who was already dying?

"Megan?"

His gruff voice always turned her inside out. When she looked up at him, he was watching her with an intensity that sent a tingle through her.

"I don't know." Barbara and Bobby resented the fact that Joe kept them a secret. Part of her understood their animosity. "Maybe Barbara knew that Joe had included her in the will. But what if he'd decided to change it recently? Maybe he was going to cut them out for some reason."

"And one or both of them decided to kill him before he could," Roan finished.

She nodded. "That would make sense."

Roan's wide jaw snapped tight. "If that's the case, I need proof. I doubt either one of the Lowmans are going to cop to murder."

She doubted that, too. "What's our next move?"

Roan's gaze met hers. "*We* don't have a next move, Megan. If you go around making accusations, you could get hurt."

Megan drummed her fingers on the table. She noticed Roan watching and realized how desperately she needed a manicure—the chemicals she worked with at the morgue were hell on her nails and skin—so she curled her fingers into her palms.

Still the questions she'd had since she'd first suspected poison in Joe's tox report nagged at her. She wasn't some delicate princess type who ran from trouble. When she had questions, she sought answers. It was the nature of being a scientist and doctor. "But I can't let this go, Roan."

Roan laid one big hand on top of both of hers. "Listen to me. I'm the lawman. First things first. Get that report, then call me with the results. If you confirm poison, I'll investigate."

Memories of him intimately touching her flooded her as she stared at their fingers. She wanted to relive that night. At least one more time.

But Roan quickly pulled his hand away, his jaw set hard again, his high cheekbones accentuated by the way his hair was pulled back in a leather tie. The only time he'd ever let down his guard was the night his mother died.

He obviously regretted doing it then.

But at least he hadn't thought she was crazy. If that report confirmed what she suspected, he'd investigate.

She'd have to be satisfied with that for now.

ROAN TRIED TO shake off the ridiculous need to fold Megan in his arms and ask her to go home with him. He could use the sweet release of a hot night in bed with her again.

But one look into that vulnerable face and he knew that would be a mistake. Megan was not a one night stand kind of girl.

Which made it even more awkward that he'd used her for comfort the night his mother died and never contacted her again.

She knew what she was getting into. She's a big girl.

Only she wasn't like the other women he knew. She was smart, curious, a problem solver.

And she had no idea how beautiful she was.

But her words disturbed him. She thought Joe was murdered. And she hadn't just offered some harebrained reason. She had offered a believable motive.

One he would investigate. On his own.

He didn't want her near him. She was too damn tempting.

Worse, asking questions could be dangerous.

He tossed some bills on the table to pay for the drink. "Like I said, call me when you get the results of that tox screen."

He stood, tipped his Stetson and strode through the busy bar. Music rocked the establishment, laughter and chatter filling the air. Men and women came here to unwind and hook up.

But he ignored the interested females and strode outside. His mind was already ticking away what he needed to do.

He and Maddox were still trying to figure out who set those fires. Could the same person have murdered Joe?

And then there was Barbara and Bobby Lowman…

Megan's comment about the will made him reach for his phone. He climbed in his SUV and punched Darren Bush's number, but received the lawyer's voice mail. "It's Deputy Whitefeather," he said. "Please call me as soon as possible."

He might be jumping the gun, but he'd drive out to the Lowmans' house tonight and take a look around.

MEGAN WATCHED ROAN leave with mixed emotions. She was relieved he'd taken her concerns seriously.

But disappointed that he didn't hint at wanting a personal relationship.

She blinked back tears. Good grief. She wasn't a crier. She'd learned long ago not to let rejection destroy her. Like her father said, she had brains and she'd use them to survive.

In fact, it was better she wasn't gorgeous like her sister. The cops suspected Shelly was targeted by the man who'd killed her because of her looks. Even their mother had been model pretty.

But she'd never gotten over Shelly's death and had eventually committed suicide as if Megan wasn't enough to fill the void Shelly had left.

As if she was the daughter who should have died instead of Shelly.

Bile rose to her throat at the memories, and she pushed her wine aside, then headed to the door. She elbowed her way through the crowd, ignoring catcalls from drunk cowboys as she stepped outside.

One beefy man in a big black hat grabbed her arm. "What's your hurry? Let your hair down and we could have a lot of fun."

She glared at him with her best "get lost" look. "Sorry, mister. Not interested."

His fingers tightened around her arm. "Hey, don't I know you? You're that medical examiner who sent my brother to jail."

She arched a brow, struggling to recall the details. "I'm sorry, I don't know what you're talking about."

"You don't remember? You said my brother killed this drifter and he's locked up now 'cause of you."

The hair on the back of her neck prickled. His tone reeked of bitterness. "I'm sorry for what happened to your family," she said. "But I was just doing my job."

"Well, you were wrong, lady. My brother didn't kill no one."

Megan forced herself to remain calm. "I file a report based on scientific evidence I find in the autopsy. The rest is up to the law and a jury." She yanked her arm away, then took a deep breath. "Now, good night."

He muttered a profanity as she brushed him out of the way and walked to her car. Gravel crunched beneath her boots, and she glanced over her shoulder to make sure the jerk wasn't following.

Keys already in hand, she pressed the unlock button on the key fob and slid into the driver's seat of her van. She liked driving something with room enough to carry her medical bag and a change of clothes when she worked all night.

The engine chugged to life, and she checked her rearview mirror. The man had followed her outside and was glaring at her as she disappeared.

Nerves knotted her stomach. He'd said she was wrong about his brother. Had she been wrong?

Everyone made mistakes. But she was careful about her reports.

Although sometimes her curiosity got the better of her—like now?

Was she looking for trouble regarding Joe Mc-Cullen's death when there hadn't been foul play?

ROAN PULLED INTO the driveway of Barbara's house, noting that most of the lights were off in the neighborhood. Barbara's house was dark, vacant now that she and her son were incarcerated.

He cut the lights, then glanced around the property, hoping not to alert anyone that he was nosing around. Maddox would probably be ticked off if he knew Roan was here, that he hadn't told him about his conversation with Megan.

But there was no need in stirring up Maddox's emotions over questions about his father's death unless he had some concrete evidence that Joe had been murdered.

He grabbed his flashlight and walked around to the rear, then checked the back door. He picked the lock and slipped inside. The house smelled of mildew, stale cigarette smoke and beer.

He shined the light through the kitchen, expecting to see dirty dishes, but the sink was empty and, except for a few empty beer bottles, the counter was free of clutter.

Remembering that he was searching for poison, he opened the refrigerator and scanned the contents. A milk carton, juice, soda, a head of wilted lettuce, carton of eggs, yogurt. He opened the milk and gagged at the sour smell.

But he saw nothing inside that looked like poison.

Next he checked the cabinets, searching below the sink, and found household cleaners, some of which were poisonous, but was it the poison that had allegedly killed Joe?

He quickly cataloged the contents of the cabinet, then searched the living room, the closet, bedrooms and bathrooms. More cleaner in the bathroom, but nothing suspicious per se.

Of course Barbara could easily have had time to dispose of the poison.

Although in light of the fact that no one had questioned Joe's cause of death, she might not have bothered. Some people were cocky enough to think they'd never get caught.

Working on that theory, he checked the bathroom garbage cans, then the kitchen. Beer cans, an empty pizza box, other assorted trash.

Frustrated, he eased out the back door and checked the outside garbage can. Only one bag of garbage, which surprised him, but before he went through it, he noticed the storage shed behind the house.

Sensing he was on to something, he picked the lock on the shed. When he opened it, he shined his flashlight across the interior and noticed several bags of potting soil, planters and gardening tools.

A storage bin sat to the right, and he lifted the lid and illuminated it with the flashlight beam.

Fertilizer.

His pulse hammered as past cases of poisoning played in his head. Fertilizers contained cyanide.

Chapter Three

Roan snapped pictures of the fertilizer bags and other assorted chemicals inside the shed, but he was careful not to touch anything. If they learned that Joe McCullen was murdered, he'd have to go by the book and gather evidence.

But the fact that Barbara had products containing cyanide definitely put her on his suspect list.

He had no idea how she got the poison into Joe, though. Had she laced food or a drink with it? That would be the most common or easiest way.

If so, that meant she had to have had access to him, had to have visited him.

Maddox might know. But Roan wasn't ready to discuss the situation with him.

He noted a pair of gardening gloves, then a box of disposable latex gloves and took a picture of the box. A lot of people bought those disposable gloves for cleaning, but Barbara could have used them when preparing whatever concoction she'd used to hide the cyanide.

He was jumping to conclusions, he realized. Just

because Barbara had motive didn't mean she was the only one who wanted Joe dead.

Arlis Bennett at the Circle T was suspected of hiring someone to set the fires on behalf of himself and his cousin, Boyle Gates. Gates had been furious at Maddox for arresting him for cattle rustling.

But the timing was off. Gates hadn't been caught until after Joe's death.

Although, what if Joe had figured out what Gates was doing?

Gates could have poisoned Joe, hoping whatever Joe had on him would die with his death.

Knowing it was too late to question either of them tonight, he mentally filed his questions for the next day.

He locked the shed as he left, once again surveying the yard and property as he walked back to his vehicle. But as he drove away from the house, his mind turned from murder to Megan.

Seeing her tonight had resurrected memories of the one night they'd spent together.

How could the worst day of his life also be one of the best?

Losing his mother had been so painful he'd allowed himself to drown his sorrows in Megan's sweet body. Her erotic touches had assuaged his anguish and helped him forget for a moment that the only person he'd ever loved, the only person who'd ever given a damn about him, was gone.

Forever.

Although, maybe he'd only perceived the night with Megan was so special because he'd been in pain…

That had to be it. If they slept together again, he'd probably be disappointed.

Perspiration rolled down his neck as he crossed through town, then veered down the drive to his cabin and parked. He climbed out, the wind rustling the trees, the sound of a coyote echoing from somewhere nearby.

Shoulders squared, he let himself inside the cabin, the cold empty room a reminder that he was alone.

Sometimes, he imagined walking in and seeing Megan in his kitchen or in his den. But most often he imagined her in his bedroom.

Waking up with Megan in his arms that night had been pure bliss. But when he'd looked at her sweet innocent face, the guilt had overwhelmed him.

Guilt for feeling pleasure when his mother had died. Then guilt for taking advantage of Megan.

Because he'd known that she wasn't the type of woman to hook up on a whim. That she might perceive their night of sex as the beginning of something—maybe a long-term relationship.

And he couldn't go there. Couldn't care about anyone.

Losing them hurt too damn much.

Just like he wouldn't allow himself to care about

the McCullens. Sure, he'd find Joe's murderer—*if* he was murdered—but then he'd step away.

And the McCullens would never know his secret.

THE NEXT MORNING, Megan couldn't shake her encounter from the night before with the man outside The Silver Bullet. Pistol Whip was a small town, but she worked for the county hospital and medical examiner's office, which covered a much larger territory.

Her boss and the senior medical examiner Frank Mantle had overseen all her cases the first year, but now he pretty much left her alone. He was nearing retirement age, suffered from arthritis and wanted to spend more time with his wife, so Megan shouldered the majority of the autopsies.

She struggled to recall the case the man she'd run into was talking about, then searched through her files. The fifth file she pulled had to be it.

The murdered man's name was Carlton Langer. He was twenty-five, just graduated from college and was traveling across country to sow his oats before he settled into a full-time job.

She rubbed her forehead as she recalled the details of the case. Carlton had been brutally stabbed three times in the chest. The knife had sliced his aorta and he'd bled out immediately.

Judging from the angle of the blade and the fact that the knife was missing, she'd had to rule it a homicide. She turned to her computer and pulled up the news reports that had followed the stabbing and noted that a man named Tad Hummings had been arrested the day after the brutal assault.

According to the officer who arrested him, Hummings had been high on drugs and the murder weapon had been found in his house with his fingerprints on it. Later, when he'd come down off the drugs, he didn't remember anything.

She rubbed her temple. It sounded as if he'd blacked out. She read the drug tox screen. Cocaine.

His brother Dale had hired a lawyer who'd argued that the drugs had caused Hummings's erratic, violent behavior.

But a man was still dead, and Tad Hummings was sent to prison.

She closed the file. Dale Hummings blamed her, but she hadn't made a mistake. His brother had. There was no question about Langer's cause of death, either.

Joe McCullen was a different story. She picked up the phone to call Howard and see if he'd finished that tox screen.

ROAN DROVE TOWARD the prison where Barbara had been incarcerated. He might be jumping the gun, but he'd always suspected she'd lied about setting the fires on Horseshoe Creek.

A cigarette butt had been found in the ashes of the barn fire, the same brand she smoked.

His phone buzzed. Maddox. "Deputy White-feather."

"I got a lead on Romley. He was spotted in Cheyenne. I'm on my way to check it out. You're in charge."

Stan Romley worked for Gates and Arlis Bennett and had taken a job at Horseshoe Creek to spy on the McCullens.

"I've got it covered," Roan said, although he was thirty miles from town. But if anything came up, he'd rush back.

"Call me if you need backup," Roan said.

Maddox agreed and hung up. Roan pulled up to the guard's station and identified himself. The guard waved him through and he parked. The wind howled as he waited outside to enter, then it took him another ten minutes to clear security.

Barbara had been placed in a minimum-security prison to serve out her year sentence for aggravated assault against the sheriff and against Scarlet Lovett. She'd cut the brake lines on the woman's car, and Scarlet had nearly been killed when she crashed into the side of the social services building where she worked.

Barbara had pled out to a lesser sentence and had to sign an agreement that she wouldn't file for an appeal in return.

He took a seat at the visitor's station, and a guard

escorted Barbara to a chair facing him through a Plexiglas partition. A seed of sympathy for her sprouted inside him—he knew the story. She and Joe McCullen had had an affair when Maddox and his brothers were children, and she'd gotten pregnant with Bobby.

When Joe's wife, Grace, had died in a car accident, Barbara had no doubt expected Joe to marry her. But that hadn't happened. Her bitterness had festered. When Joe died, she'd hoped her son would inherit his share of Horseshoe Creek.

Joe had included him in the will, but neither Barbara nor Bobby were satisfied.

The woman looked pale and angry, her dyed blond hair now mixed with muddy brown. For a moment, she studied him, obviously wondering what his agenda was.

She'd been volatile when she was arrested. Prison had drained the fight from her.

He picked up the phone and waited until she did the same.

"Ms. Lowman," he began. "Thank you for seeing me."

She shrugged, her eyes fixed on him. "Didn't realize I had a choice."

No, she was at the mercy of the justice system now. "How are you?"

She frowned. "What? Like you care?"

She was right. He didn't really care. She'd tried

to kill an innocent woman. Scarlet was one of the nicest people he'd ever met.

"Why are you really here, Deputy?" Barbara asked.

Roan narrowed his eyes. "I thought you might be ready to tell the truth about the fires at Horseshoe Creek. I could speak to the judge on your behalf and arrange an early parole if you confess."

Barbara's sarcastic laugh echoed over the line. "Right. I confess to another crime and you'll get me out of here earlier? What kind of fool do you think I am?"

"I don't think you're a fool at all," Roan said. "I think you resented Joe for not marrying you, especially after you waited for him all these years."

"Who said I waited for him?"

"You never married." He leaned closer to the Plexiglass. "Did you even date anyone else, Barbara? Or did you sit at home hoping he'd call?" He lowered his voice, taunting her. "Did you keep thinking that next month or next year he'd finally admit that he loved you and make you his wife?"

Barbara's nostrils flared. "How dare you."

"I understand your anger," Roan continued. "You gave Joe a son just like Grace did, but her sons got to live on the big ranch. They got to have Joe's name and grow up in the house with him. They got a real father. Yet McCullen kept you and Bobby on the side. Made you live in the shadows and take whatever little pieces he had left over from his real family." He paused for effect. "He was ashamed of the two of you."

She lurched up, body shaking with fury. "You bastard. Joe loved me and Bobby."

"If he'd loved you, he would have introduced you to his sons. He would have married you." Roan remained seated, his expression calm, his eyes scrutinizing her. "But he didn't, and every day, every month, every year that went by, your bitterness grew. Then…what happened? Maybe you gave him an ultimatum, that you'd expose him to Maddox and Brett and Ray, if he didn't marry you."

"That's ridiculous," Barbara said, although the guilt that flashed in her eyes indicated he'd hit the nail on the head.

He raised a brow. "But he still refused. That must have torn you up inside."

Barbara sank into the chair again and looked down at the floor, her face wrenched in pain. "He felt guilty about his wife's death. That's why he never married me. Even from the grave she kept her tentacles embedded in him."

"Then you finally snapped, didn't you, Barbara. You decided that if he wouldn't marry you, you'd get rid of him. At least then you and your son could get what he owed you."

"He did owe us," Barbara snapped. "We loved him and kept his secret to protect him, and he still let us down."

"That was the final straw, wasn't it?" Roan said.

"He refused to marry you. Maybe he even said he'd never marry you." He arched a brow. "Maybe he threatened to cut you out of the will."

Her chin lifted and tears glittered in her eyes.

"So you decided to get rid of him. He was sick already so you poisoned him. Nice and slow, just a little at a time."

"What?" Barbara's jaw went slack. "Poisoned Joe?"

"Yes. Did you take him food or a drink when you visited him? Did you slowly poison him and watch him die?"

Barbara's face blanched. "What are you saying? That Joe was murdered?"

"You tell me, Ms. Lowman. Did you kill Joe Mc-Cullen?"

MEGAN CLOSED THE door to her office as she waited on the lab to answer. Finally Howard picked up. "Howard, it's Megan."

"I was just getting ready to call you," Howard said.

"Did you finish the tests?"

"Yes. Meet me at the coffee shop across from the hospital."

"I'm on my way." Megan snatched her purse, hurried from her office and locked the door behind her. She caught the elevator from the basement floor where the morgue was housed, then wove through the corridors of the hospital past the gift shop and outside. She had to cross the street to the corner café.

By the time she arrived, Howard was ordering coffee. She ordered a latte and then they claimed a booth in the back corner.

"What did you find?" she asked, unable to stand the wait.

Howard glanced around the coffee shop, then spoke in a hushed tone. "You were right, Megan. There were definitely traces of cyanide in McCullen's system."

Megan's pulse pounded. That meant Joe was murdered.

"What are you going to do with this information?" Howard asked.

Megan blew the steam rolling off her coffee. "I have to go to the police." In fact, she already had.

"Joe was the sheriff's father, right?"

"Yes." And she had no idea how he would react.

"Didn't the sheriff live with his father?" Howard asked.

Megan frowned. "Yes."

"How did someone poison his old man without him knowing it?"

"I have no idea, but I know someone who'll find out." She pulled her phone from her purse and punched Roan's number. His phone rolled to voice mail, and she left a message for him to call her.

"What about Dr. Cumberland?" Howard asked.

"He was close to Joe, but with Joe's illness, I guess he never thought to look for another cause."

"You'll tell him?" Howard asked.

"Of course." She didn't look forward to it, either, not after the way he'd reacted when she'd questioned the tox screen.

They finished their coffee and Howard had to rush back to the lab. She lingered, hoping Roan would return her call, but finally decided to go back to work. When she stepped outside, a chilly wind rippled through the air. The sky was dark with clouds, although it hadn't rained in days.

She shivered, and had an eerie feeling as if someone was watching her. Remembering her encounter with Hummings's brother the night before, she checked around her as she walked to the crosswalk, but she didn't spot the man anywhere.

She stepped up to the street where a group had gathered waiting on the traffic signal. Her phone rang just as the light turned. She pressed Answer and fell into step with the crowd, but suddenly a gunshot blasted the air. The crowd screamed and began to run, and she felt someone shove her from behind, then lost her balance.

She landed on her hands and knees, and her phone went flying across the street.

She looked up and screamed as an oncoming car screeched toward her.

Chapter Four

Roan studied Barbara for a reaction. She seemed shocked at his accusation. "Did you poison Joe McCullen, Barbara?"

Barbara's handcuffs jangled as she waved her hands dramatically in the air. "Of course not. I can't believe you'd ask me such a thing. I loved that man more than life itself."

"You loved him, but we both know you resented the fact that he never married you."

Barbara looked down at the jagged ends of her nails. "Did someone really poison him?"

"There were traces of cyanide in his system."

She jerked her gaze up, eyes flaring with surprise. Or guilt? "Cyanide?"

"Yes. Fertilizer has cyanide in it, Barbara. And you have plenty of that at your house. You use it in your gardening."

Another flicker of unease in her eyes. Then she seemed to pull herself together. "Gardening was a hobby of mine. But a lot of people garden. That's not a crime."

"No, but slipping cyanide into food or a drink that someone ingests is."

"I didn't slip cyanide into anything."

Roan worked his mouth from side to side. "Then maybe your son did."

Anger slashed her tired-looking features. "My son did no such thing."

Roan arched a brow. "Are you sure about that, Barbara? He resented Joe more than you did. He hated all of the McCullens. Maybe he even went to see Joe and Joe told him not to come back, that he didn't want his real sons to know about him." He paused. "Maybe he told Bobby that he'd never be a McCullen. That if he got any of the land, he'd have to work underneath Maddox like he was some kind of servant."

Barbara shot up. "Stop it. Joe wouldn't have talked to Bobby like that. He loved our son."

"But not like he did Maddox or Brett or Ray," Roan pressed.

Rage darkened Barbara's eyes. "Listen to me, Deputy. Bobby and I have suffered enough. We have both been locked up because of that family, but we did not kill Joe. Now leave us alone."

She whirled around and gestured toward the guard. "Take me back to my cell, please."

The guard glanced at Roan, and he shrugged and gestured okay. But before Barbara stepped through the door, he cleared his throat. "Know this, Barbara.

If you or Bobby did kill Joe, I'll find out. And any chance of you getting free will disappear."

She shot him a venomous look, then shuffled out the door with the guard.

Roan contemplated her reaction.

Had she been so desperate to protect her son and see him get what was owed to him that she killed the man she loved?

MEGAN'S HEART HAMMERED as tires squealed and the car roared toward her. Terrified for her life, she rolled sideways toward the sidewalk seconds before the car screeched to a stop.

If she hadn't been so fast, the car would have hit her.

Her life flashed in front of her. Playing with her sister when she was little. Losing her. Losing her mother… Her father looking at her like she was nothing.

Being so lonely sometimes she thought she'd die…

Then that night with Roan…his handsome face. Him bending over her, making love to her.

She wanted to live, to be with him again.

Shouts and screams echoed around her, then a man raced to her and helped her up. "Are you all right, miss?"

The driver of the car jumped out, the woman's face ashen as she stumbled toward Megan. "Oh, God, honey, are you okay?"

"Yes," Megan said. She glanced around the street and saw several people watching while others had dispersed in fear. "Someone fired a gun."

"I heard it," the man who'd helped her up said. "But I didn't see where it came from."

"I think it was a car backfiring," a gray-haired man said.

"No, no, it was definitely a gun," another woman said.

Megan didn't know what to think. But…she'd also thought she'd felt someone push her before she fell.

You're just being paranoid.

Although she had expressed suspicions about Joe McCullen's death, the only people who knew that were Howard and Roan. And they were on her side.

Of course Tad Hummings's brother had cornered her in the bar—would he try to kill her because she'd helped send his brother to prison?

"Are you sure you don't need an ambulance?" the driver of the car asked.

"I'm sure." All she wanted to do was call Roan. Then hide in the morgue where she was safe.

Except she needed to talk to Dr. Cumberland. And he wasn't going to like what she had to say.

ROAN CONSIDERED QUESTIONING Bobby but decided he needed concrete proof before he did. Something that would force Bobby to confess.

He climbed in his SUV to leave the prison and phoned Megan as he drove onto the highway. Her phone rang three times before she answered. When she did, she sounded breathless.

"Megan, are you all right?"

"No. I mean, yes," she said. "I'm on the way back to the morgue."

"What's wrong?"

"I went to meet Howard to discuss the tox results, but on the way back to the hospital a gunshot sounded. The crowd panicked and started running, and I fell in the street."

Roan went very still. "You fell?"

"Yes, well, I don't know. I thought for a minute I was pushed, but I could have imagined it. Everyone was running to get away."

"Who fired the gun?"

'I have no idea," she said. "The street was crowded and it happened so fast. One man said he thought it was a car backfiring, but I don't think so."

"Did you see anyone suspicious?"

"No. But like I said, it happened really fast and a car was coming so I had to roll out of the way."

He didn't like this one damn bit. First, she'd come to him questioning Joe McCullen's death. Now a gun had gone off in the street and she'd fallen and nearly been hit by a car.

Too coincidental.

Roan clenched the phone with clammy hands. "Who else did you tell about the tox report?"

Tension filled the air. "Just you and Howard, the lab tech and Dr. Cumberland. But I haven't seen him since I met with Howard earlier."

"What were the results?"

"There was definitely cyanide in Joe's system, Roan. Probably administered in small doses over a long period of time so as not to draw suspicion."

Roan veered onto the road leading toward the McCullens' ranch, Horseshoe Creek. He needed to find out who'd visited Joe on a regular basis.

"I know this will upset Dr. Cumberland," Megan said. "He and the McCullens are good friends."

"So how did he miss the fact that his patient was poisoned?"

"Like I said, it was probably administered in slow doses. Since Joe was already ill, Dr. Cumberland must have assumed his weakening condition was due to the disease."

Roan's mind raced. Barbara was his prime suspect, but her shock had seemed real. "But one question is still bothering me—why kill a dying man?"

"Maybe Barbara and Bobby knew about the will, but thought Joe was going to change it and take them out. She could have wanted him dead before he could make the change."

"That's possible. I put a call in to Joe's lawyer to find out."

His phone beeped. Maddox. "Listen, Megan, Maddox is calling. Let me talk to him."

"Are you going to tell him his father was murdered?"

Roan hesitated. That was not a conversation he was eager to have.

"Not yet. I want some proof of a viable suspect before I go to him."

"I don't blame you. The McCullens have been through a lot. But they will want to know."

He was well aware of that. "Don't worry. I'll tell him when the time is right." He hesitated, then remembered her close call on the street. "Be careful, Megan. And don't talk to anyone but Dr. Cumberland about this."

She agreed, and he hit Connect to respond to Maddox. "It's Roan."

"I think I've tracked Romley down. I'm staking out a motel where he was last spotted."

"Do you need backup?"

"Not yet. I'll let you know if I do. Is anything going on there?"

Roan swallowed hard. He hated to lie, but…he wasn't ready to divulge the truth. "No. I'll ride out and check on the ranch soon."

"Thanks. That security detail Brett hired should have it covered. But I'm worried about Mama Mary and Rose staying at the house while I'm gone. I tried to get them to stay with a friend, but they're both as stubborn as they come. Mama Mary said no one would run her off from her home, and Rose insisted on staying with her."

"Don't worry. I'll check on them." In fact, Mama Mary was the one person who'd been by Joe's bedside when he was ill. She'd lived with the family since before the boys' mother passed and was the cook, housekeeper and surrogate mother. According to Maddox, she was as much a part of the family as anyone.

She would know exactly who'd visited Joe. And if he had other enemies, she could provide them with a list of names.

MEGAN COULDN'T SHAKE the uneasy feeling that someone had meant to harm her in the street.

The man from the bar, Tad Hummings's brother?

She should report her altercation with him to the police. To Roan.

But…she had no real proof that he'd pushed her today. And he was already angry with her over the injustice he'd perceived she'd done to his family. If she accused him of pushing her in front of a car or firing a weapon at her, he would be furious.

She didn't want to deal with that kind of rage. Or to falsely accuse anyone of anything.

She finished filing the results on Morty Burns and sent them to the sheriff in Laredo. This was his case, not one for Roan or Sheriff McCullen. But she was curious about the man so she entered his name in her database and ran a background check.

Information filled the screen.

Morty Burns, age fifty-nine, five-ten, a hundred and ninety pounds, no preexisting conditions.

He was married to a woman named Edith Bennett.

Bennett—why did that name sound familiar?

A knock sounded at her office door, but before she could respond, Dr. Cumberland stormed in.

"What the hell are you doing, Megan?" He slashed his hand through the air. "I just found out you ran more labs on Joe McCullen. I thought we settled that issue."

Megan pivoted, forcing a calm to her voice.

She hadn't let her father intimidate her and she wouldn't let this man.

"I'm sorry, Doctor, but the fact that there were two different results bugged me. So I decided to run it one more time."

Dr. Cumberland rammed his hands through his hair, spiking the white strands in disarray. "I can't believe you'd go behind my back—"

"This is not about you," Megan said. "It's about your good friend Joe. If someone did hurt him, wouldn't you want to know?"

"Of course," he stuttered.

"I still don't understand about the false negative."

Dr. Cumberland looked away. "Sometimes our samples get contaminated and it throws off the results."

That had happened before. "I know you cared

about him," Megan said softly. "And so did his sons. I just want the truth."

He paused in his pacing and turned to look at her, his expression pained. "What are you saying, Megan? That someone killed my best and oldest friend? That it happened while he was under my care?"

Chapter Five

Dr. Cumberland looked completely distraught.

Megan stepped over to him and squeezed his shoulder. "I'm sorry, Doctor, I know this is upsetting."

The man's face contorted with emotions. "How could I have missed that? I saw him all the time…"

"It happened so slowly, there was no reason for you to look for it, not with Joe already dying."

"This makes no sense," he said. "Why would anyone kill Joe? He didn't have long to live."

"That's the big question," Megan said. "And one I'm sure his sons will want the answer to."

Dr. Cumberland looked stricken, and then he slumped into a chair and dropped his head into his hands. "Good God, Joe…what have I done?"

The guilt in the man's voice tugged at Megan's heartstrings. "You didn't do anything. Joe knew you were his friend. If he'd thought someone was poisoning him, he would have told you."

"But I was his primary physician. I should have realized, should have seen something."

"Like I said, whoever poisoned him did it in small doses over a long period of time." She drummed her fingers on the desk. "Can you think of anyone who had a grudge against Joe?"

"Just Barbara. And maybe Arlis Bennett, but he's in jail." He pushed himself up, but staggered slightly. His pallor was gray, his breathing unsteady.

Megan reached out to steady him. "Are you okay? You aren't having chest pains, are you?"

He shook his head no, then straightened and swiped at the perspiration beading on his forehead. "I have to go."

"Wait." She caught his arm. "Maybe you need to see a doctor."

"I'm fine, I just need some air." He shrugged off her hand and hurried toward the door before she could stop him.

Roan's gut churned with the news of Joe McCullen's murder.

For a fraction of a second, he considered the possibility that this could have been a mercy killing. Mama Mary supposedly loved the McCullens like family—she'd taken care of Joe during his illness.

What if she'd hated seeing him suffer and decided to speed death along?

Although slowly poisoning someone was not merciful. If Mama Mary or someone else, say Dr.

Cumberland, had wanted to keep Joe from suffering, he or she would have found a faster way.

As he drove down the long winding drive to the main farmhouse at Horseshoe Creek, he scanned the property. It was an impressive spread. Now it belonged to Joe's three sons.

Horses galloped across the fields while cattle grazed in the pastures. Brett had brought more horses in to train and planned to offer riding lessons and was rebuilding the barns that burned down. He'd taken his wife, Willow, and his son away for a couple of weeks in hopes Maddox would track down the culprit sabotaging the McCullens.

Hopefully Maddox would arrest Romley and the trouble would end.

But the fact that Joe had been murdered changed everything. Was Gates responsible? Or… Barbara or Bobby?

Sunshine slanted across the graveled drive and farmhouse as he parked. The ground was dry from lack of rain, although winds stirred dust and scattered leaves and twigs across the yard. Hopefully spring would come soon with warmer weather, new growth and the ranch could get back on track.

But he wouldn't be a part of it. He didn't belong.

Still, he had to get justice for his father.

The sound of cattle echoed above the low whine of the wind, and he spotted a cowboy at the top of the hill herding the cows toward the pasture to the east.

A gray cloud moved across the sky shrouding the sun as he strode up to the front porch.

He knocked, noting that the repairs on the house were complete.

He knocked again, then heard shuffling inside. "Hang on to your britches, I'm coming."

Roan shifted and scanned the perimeter of the property again, searching for anyone lurking around, but nothing suspicious stood out. A second later, Mama Mary lumbered to the door and opened it.

The scent of cinnamon wafted toward Roan, making his mouth water.

The short, chubby lady wiped her hands on her apron as she invited him in. She'd wound a bandana around her chin-length brown curls and flour dusted her blouse and apron. Her brown eyes were so warm and loving that Roan couldn't help but envy the McCullens. Although alarm tinged them at the sight of him. "Deputy Whitefeather, Is something wrong? Did you hear from Maddox?"

"Maddox is fine," Roan assured her. "I spoke to him earlier today. He has a lead on Stan Romley."

Relief softened her face. "Thank goodness. Maybe they'll lock him up, and my boys can get back to work here on the ranch where they belong."

Her boys. She said it with such affection that if he'd ever considered the possibility of her doing something to hurt the family, that thought vanished like dust in the wind.

"May I come in? I'd like to ask you some questions."

Her eyes narrowed. "Something is wrong. Something you don't want to say."

Roan jammed his hands in his pockets. She was damned intuitive. "I'm just trying to help Maddox identify the arsonist."

She nodded, although she scrutinized his face as if she didn't quite believe him. Still, she waved him in. "You want some tea or coffee?"

"Coffee would be good," he said. Maybe it would put them both at ease if he at least acted like this was informal, not a hunting expedition. Although, if she knew her boss and family friend had been murdered, he had a feeling she would want to help.

She gestured toward the den where a fire crackled in the fireplace, and she disappeared into the kitchen while he surveyed the room. A family picture of Joe and his three sons hung on one wall— the boys were teenagers then. A bookshelf held other pictures, a couple of Joe and the woman who must have been his wife, Grace. A third one showed Grace holding a baby in her arms with two toddlers beside her—Ray had to be the baby, Maddox and Brett the toddlers.

How would she have reacted if she'd known that

Joe had another son at that time? Roan was probably just a few months older than Maddox.

His hand stroked his wallet where he kept a picture of his mother. There had been no father in the picture because she'd chosen not to tell Joe about him. What would Joe have done if he'd known? Would he have offered to marry Roan's mother?

Would he have grown up a McCullen and lived on a ranch like this?

A wave of disappointment hit him, but he tamped it back. No use wondering. It hadn't happened.

Footsteps sounded, and Mama Mary waddled in carrying a tray with a coffee craft, two mugs and a plate of cinnamon rolls. She set them on the coffee table, handed him a plate with a cinnamon roll on it, then served them both a mug and offered cream and sugar.

"Black is fine," he said as he cradled the warm mug in his hand. Even the coffee cups had an *M* on them for McCullen, another reminder that if his mother had married Joe, that would have been his last name, too.

Mama Mary studied him with a frown. "All right, what's really going on, Deputy? Maddox is after Romley and we know that he worked for Boyle Gates, the man Maddox put away for cattle rustling. I'm aware you all looked into his cousin Bennett. Do you have new information?"

He sipped his coffee, choosing his words carefully. "We're still hoping that Romley will give us a confession regarding the fires."

"So why are you here?"

Roan nodded. "The last few months Joe was sick, Dr. Cumberland came often to check on him?"

She nodded, then stirred sugar into her coffee. "Almost every day. He and Joe went way back. He even delivered Joe's boys."

Except for him. And Bobby. But they obviously didn't count. "Joe and Boyle Gates had trouble?"

Mama Mary sighed. "Well, I guess you could say that. Boyle tried to get Joe to sell some of his land to him. He wasn't happy at all when Joe refused."

"Did Gates visit Joe while he was sick?"

Mama Mary nodded. "A couple of times. I couldn't believe he kept persisting. He must have thought that Joe was weak and would give in, but Joe was adamant that his ranch belonged to the McCullens and didn't intend to let any of it go."

Gates would have had to have administered the poison more than twice for it to show up in the tox screen. Maybe he hired someone to sneak it into Joe's food or drink?

"How about other visitors?"

"Well, a few of the hands dropped by. The foreman and Joe were close. He stopped in at least once a week."

"You said they were close? Did he have any trouble with Joe?"

"No, Joe was always good to him. They were

more like brothers than employee-employer." She made a clicking sound with her teeth. "Why are you asking about Mr. Joe's visitors?"

"I'm trying to get the full picture of anyone involved with the ranch or Joe. It's possible Gates paid someone other than Romley to sabotage the ranch."

She chewed on her bottom lip and looked away. "Mr. Brett already checked out the hands. Romley turned out to be dirty, and Maddox found out he was working with another hand named Hardwick. They were both on Gates's payroll."

"What about visitors outside the ranch? Other than Dr. Cumberland, who came to see Joe while he was sick?"

She set her coffee on the tray and rubbed at her knee as if it hurt. "Barbara stopped by a few times, always when Maddox wasn't around. Once I heard her up there crying over him. I tried to stay out of the way when she was here. She didn't much care for me."

"She was bitter," Roan said. "Did she bring Joe any gifts or food when she visited?"

Mama Mary's face crinkled as she scrunched her nose in thought. "Sometimes she brought him cookies. Said they were his favorites, that she made them for him the first time they met."

"Did Joe eat them?"

"One or two here and there. To tell you the truth,

he wasn't into sweets that much. He was a meat and potato man."

Still, she could have poisoned the cookies.

"What about Bobby? Did he visit Joe?"

She scoffed. "That boy was like vinegar, sour and bitter as they get. He came some, but I stayed out of his way. He upset Mr. Joe. Sometimes I could hear them shouting all the way in the kitchen." She made a sound of disapproval. "When Joe took sick, you'd have thought Bobby would have softened and been nicer. But one night I heard him asking Joe when he was going to tell the other boys about him. He was always demanding money, too."

Roan's pulse jumped. "What about Joe's will? Did Bobby know he was included?"

"Joe hinted that he'd included him, but more than once he told Bobby if he wanted any part of the Mc-Cullen land, he had to get help."

Roan considered their argument. "Did Joe ever talk about changing his will?"

Mama Mary glanced down at her fingers where she was knotting the apron in her lap. "He did. I told him once he should take that boy out. He was ungrateful and a mean drunk, and he didn't deserve what Joe had worked so hard for."

"Did Joe talk to the lawyer about it?"

"I honestly don't know," Mama Mary said with a sigh.

There was one way to find out. Roan had to talk to Joe's lawyer Darren Bush.

MEGAN SPENT THE rest of the afternoon working on the autopsy of a car crash victim.

By late afternoon, she was so concerned about the doctor that she phoned him to make certain he didn't need medical attention, but his voice mail kicked in. Her phone buzzed a second later.

Thinking it was him, she quickly snatched up the phone.

"Dr. Lail, this is Deputy North in Laredo. I got the results for that autopsy on Morty Burns."

"Yes."

"Did you find any forensics?"

"I'm afraid not," Megan answered. "But the bullet that killed him was from a .45."

"Hmm."

"Something bothering you about the report?" she asked.

"Not the report per se. But I talked to Sheriff McCullen from Pistol Whip. Apparently Morty Burns was married to a woman named Edith Bennett."

"Yes, I saw that," Megan said.

Deputy North grunted. "Well, her brother is Arlis Bennett, a man the sheriff suspects is working with Boyle Gates."

There was the name Bennett again. "Has Burns's wife been notified of his death?" Megan asked.

"Not yet," the deputy said. "I phoned and there was no answer at her place. She lives near Pistol Whip, not Laredo."

Megan drummed her fingers on the desk. "I can go out and talk to her."

"We really should have an officer present. This is a murder investigation now."

"All right, I'll get Deputy Whitefeather to accompany me."

"Good. Sheriff McCullen thinks Burns's murder may be related to the trouble at his ranch. That he might have been paid to set the ranch fires and that he might have been killed to cover up what he did." He paused. "Anyway, I was hoping you'd found some DNA to tie his death to Gates or Bennett."

"I'm sorry, I wish I could tell you more."

He thanked her and hung up, and Megan stewed over the information.

It hadn't occurred to her that a murder victim who'd been on her table might be connected to the McCullens.

She texted Roan to relay the deputy's statement and explained that she'd meet him at the woman's home to make the death notification—and question the woman in case she knew who'd taken her husband's life. There was always the possibility that this murder was not related to the McCullens, that it was a domestic dispute gone bad or that Burns had gotten himself in some kind of trouble. Maybe he owed someone money...

Her phone beeped indicating a response to her text, and she read Roan's message. At Horseshoe

Creek now. Will meet you at the Burns farm. Wait for me.

She texted back OK, then grabbed her purse and rushed down the hallway.

Outside, the sun was setting, storm clouds rolling in, the wind picking up. The parking lot at the hospital was still full, though; the afternoon-evening shift hadn't arrived, and an ambulance was rolling up.

She hit the key fob to unlock her car, jumped in and headed toward the address for the Burnses' farm.

Traffic was thin as she drove through town, the diner starting to fill up with the early supper crowd. She made the turn to the highway leading out of Pistol Whip, and ten minutes later found the farm, a run-down-looking piece of property that had seen better days.

Overgrown weeds choked what had once been a big garden area, the fences were broken and rotting and the house needed paint badly. Her car rumbled over the ruts in the dirt drive, dust spewing in a smoky cloud behind her.

She scanned the property for life, for workers, but saw no one. Just a deserted tractor and pickup truck in front of the weathered house. She parked and glanced around, suddenly nervous.

She didn't know anything about this woman, except that her husband had been murdered.

Suddenly the door on the side inched open and a

cat darted out. Megan's stomach knotted when she noticed blood on the cat's fur and paws.

Fear momentarily immobilized her, but her instinct as a doctor kicked in, and she threw the door open and climbed from her car. She scanned the area for someone suspicious but saw no one. The cat ran into the barn behind the house.

She eased to the porch, one hand on the mace in her purse, her phone at her fingertips in case she needed to call for help. Wind beat at the house, banging a shutter that had come loose against the weathered wood.

She crept up the rickety steps, the squeaking sound of rotting boards adding to her frayed nerves. By the time she reached the front door, perspiration trickled down the back of her neck. Senses honed, she paused to listen for sounds inside.

The wind whistled through the eaves. Water dripped from a faucet or tub somewhere in the house.

The smell of something acrid swirled in the air as she poked her head inside. The living room with its faded and tattered furniture was empty. She took a deep breath and inched inside the door.

A sick feeling swept over her when she spotted the woman lying in the doorway from the kitchen to the den.

She lay in a pool of blood, one arm outstretched as if she was reaching for help, her eyes wide-open and filled with the shock of death.

Chapter Six

Roan polished off the cinnamon roll and thanked Mama Mary. It was the best thing he'd ever tasted. "Mama Mary," Roan said. "Do you know a man named Morty Burns?"

"Can't say as I do," she said with a puzzled look. "Should I?"

Roan shrugged. "How about a woman named Edith Bennett? She was married to Burns."

Mama Mary frowned. "Bennett? Why, yes, Edith used to be good friends with Grace. Although her brother is Arlis Bennett? And she did used to visit Joe from time to time. Why?"

"That text was the ME's office. Edith's husband was found shot to death. I wondered if he worked for Bennett."

She fluttered a pudgy hand to her cheek. "Well… I don't know. I can't imagine Edith and her husband doing something illegal. You think someone killed him because he was sabotaging Horseshoe Creek?"

"At this point, I'm considering all angles." He folded his hands. "Who else visited Joe?"

Mama Mary wiped her hands on her apron again. "Hmm, well there was another rancher named Elmore Clark. He owed Joe 'cause he got in trouble with his mortgage and Joe bought some of his land to help him out."

"So he had no reason to hurt Joe?"

Mama Mary shook her head no. "Not that I'm aware of."

Roan would check out the man. Maybe he hadn't liked the terms of the sale?

"Did Joe tell you how he'd structured things in his will?"

Mama Mary brushed at the specks of flour on her apron. "Not the specifics. He just said everyone in the family would be taken care of." She made a low sound in her throat. "I urged him to talk to the boys about Barbara and Bobby, but he had so much guilt over the affair he'd had. And frankly I think he was too weak to face the hurt he'd see on their faces."

"So you knew about Barbara when he had the affair?"

She blinked and looked away. "I'm not going to gossip about this family. Joe made mistakes, but he was a good man."

"I'm not judging him," Roan said, tempted to confide in her that the man had been murdered. She obviously loved Joe and would want the truth.

Although she was protective of the family and probably wouldn't welcome him into it any more than Maddox or Brett or Ray. "Neither am I, Mama

Mary. I'm simply trying to understand the situation so we can catch whoever is sabotaging Horseshoe Creek."

She relaxed a little. "Barbara and Bobby and Boyle Gates are the only three I can think of."

Maybe he should have a chat with Boyle Gates. His phone buzzed and he checked the number. Megan.

"Thanks, Mama Mary. If you think of anyone else who visited or anything else that can help, call me."

She pushed her bulk to her feet with a heaving sound, then caught his arm as he started to stand. "Deputy Whitefeather, is there something you're not telling me?"

Roan met her gaze. Again he was tempted to confide the truth about the patriarch of the family's death. But Maddox and Brett and Ray deserved to know first. So he shook his head, punched Connect on the phone and headed out the kitchen door.

"Deputy Whitefeather."

"Roan, it's Megan… You should get out here."

His pulse hammered. "What's wrong? Where are you?"

"At the Burns farm…" Her voice cracked. "Edith Burns is dead."

MEGAN TOOK DEEP breaths as she stared at the pool of blood on the floor surrounding the woman's body.

She yanked gloves from her purse and tiptoed

inside, listening for sounds that an intruder was still there. The linoleum floor squeaked as she crossed the den to the doorway of the kitchen. She clenched the phone in one hand as she stooped down to check the woman's pulse. Not that she had any doubt that she was dead. The odors and pallor confirmed her suspicions.

But it was routine and she needed to determine time and cause of death.

"Megan, you're sure?"

"Yes." Dried blood soaked the lady's yellow housedress. "It appears that she bled out from a gunshot wound to the chest just like her husband."

"I'm on my way," Roan said. "Wait till I get there to go inside."

"I'm already inside," Megan said. "I saw blood from the doorway and had to see if she was alive."

"Dammit, Megan, what if the killer is still there?"

"He's long gone, Roan. Judging from rigor and body decomp, she's been dead several hours."

"You're alone?"

She twisted to listen for sounds again, but barring the wind battering the wood frame and windowpanes, everything was quiet. "Yes. I'll call a crime team to start processing the house."

"Do you see a bullet casing or weapon anywhere around?"

Megan lifted the woman slightly to search for an exit wound, but didn't see one. "The bullet must still be lodged inside her. I don't see a weapon anywhere."

She did a quick visual sweep of the kitchen, at least what she could see of it. A bowl of fruit sat on an oak table, fruit flies swarming. A kitchen island held a cutting board where potatoes and carrots lay, a knife on the board as if Edith had been preparing dinner when whoever killed her had struck.

From where she stood, she couldn't tell if the back door had been jimmied or if the killer had broken in.

If so, had Edith heard her attacker?

She checked the woman's fingernails, but didn't see visible signs of DNA or skin cells, but she'd scrape and run tests to make certain. No blood or hair fibers.

What about that knife? Had Edith tried to fight off her attacker with it?

She carefully stepped around her body, searching for footprints or evidence, and spotted blood splatters on the floor near the island, although the knife didn't appear to have blood on it.

She studied the kitchen layout and pieced together a feasible scenario. Perhaps the killer had entered through the back door, which meant Edith was facing away from him. But she'd been shot in the chest.

So…she must have heard a noise and turned to see what or who it was. Maybe she even knew the shooter, so she didn't instantly run.

The killer then fired the weapon. The bullet struck her heart and she grabbed the island in shock. Blood had spurted from the wound immediately, splattering droplets on the floor.

She staggered toward the den and collapsed in the threshold of the door. She was trying to go out the front…maybe to get to her car? Maybe to reach her phone and call for help?

But she'd been bleeding badly, quickly grew weak and lost consciousness before she could make it to the door or her phone.

A shiver rippled up her spine. Had the same person killed Morty Burns, then came here and shot Edith?

Or…she had to consider the possibility that it was murder-suicide. Morty could have shot Edith then left and killed himself.

Except…the timing didn't seem right. And most suicides were gunshots to the head—Morty's had been to the heart. Also, if he had committed suicide, why wouldn't he have killed himself here beside his wife?

Morty's body had been dumped…

Which brought her back to the intruder theory. What kind of cold-blooded person shot an innocent woman and simply stood there and watched her die?

And why kill either of these people? Were their deaths connected to Joe McCullen's?

QUESTIONS ASSAILED ROAN as he sped toward the Burns farm.

The fact that Edith was related to Arlis Bennett, the cousin of a man who Joe's sons had put in jail for cattle rustling, seemed too coincidental not to raise suspicions.

He had to discuss the situation with Maddox. Finding the couple's killer could be instrumental in determining who'd poisoned Joe.

Storm clouds moved in the sky, painting the run-down farm a depressing gray. The pastures and fields were overgrown, the farm equipment looked rusty and broken down and the barn needed a new roof. He saw no cattle or horses on the land, either.

Had money troubles driven Morty to help Boyle Gates or his brother-in-law sabotage Horseshoe Creek?

His police SUV rumbled and he rolled to a stop beside Megan's van. On the lookout for trouble, he scanned the perimeter of the property in case some-one was lurking nearby.

Dead leaves swirled in the wind across the brit-tle grass, and the door to the toolshed next to the house banged back and forth. An engine rumbled and he turned to see the crime team's van racing over the hill.

He glanced back at the house and saw Megan step into the doorway. Her hair was pulled back in that tight bun again, her glasses in place. Her expression was stoic, eyes dark with the reality of what she'd discovered in the house.

For a brief second, he wanted to sweep her away from the gruesomeness of her work and his job. Take her someplace cozy and romantic like a cabin in the mountains where they could float down the river on a raft then curl up on a blanket and make love beneath the stars.

Car doors slamming jerked him from the ridiculous thoughts. He was not a man who made love under the stars or…made love at all. Sex was a physical release.

It had been good with Megan. Damn good. But it wouldn't happen again.

She did her job because she liked it and was good at it just as he was good at solving crimes. Dead bodies were their life.

Not cozy mountain retreats.

"Dr. Lail called," Lieutenant Hoberman said as he and two crime techs approached. "She found a body?"

Roan nodded. "Yes, the wife of a murder victim she'd autopsied."

Lieutenant Hoberman's brows rose. "Both murdered?"

"It looks that way. Maybe you can help us pinpoint what happened."

Together they walked up the drive to the porch and climbed the steps. "You okay?" Roan asked Megan.

She gave a short nod, then led the way inside. The stench of decay filled the air, the sight of the woman's body fueling Roan's anger when he spotted her gray hair and gnarled hand reaching out as if begging for help.

Everyone pulled on latex gloves as they entered, and then they gathered around the victim. One of the crime workers began snapping photographs while the other started searching for forensics.

"It looks like she was cutting vegetables when someone entered from the back of the house," Megan said. "I think she heard the noise and turned to see who it was, then he shot her in the chest."

Poor woman was probably in her sixties. Dozens of pictures of her with a slender thirtysomething woman sat on the bookshelves. Then photos of Edith and a dark-haired boy and girl along with a card that read, "Happy Mother's Day, Grandma."

Roan's chest squeezed. She was a grandmother for God's sake.

She hadn't deserved to be gunned down in her home.

Roan's phone buzzed. Darren Bush. He excused himself and stepped on the front porch to take the call.

"Deputy Whitefeather, I got your message."

"Yes, we're still investigating the fires at Horseshoe Creek. When did Joe McCullen make his will?"

"Ten years ago, but he reviewed it each year."

"Did he make any significant changes in the last few months before his death?"

"No. Well, he did purchase a couple more plots of land. He added one of those in the settlement. It went to Bobby Lowman."

Right. "So he didn't plan to change his will and cut Barbara or Bobby out?"

"No, God no. He was adamant about taking care of his family."

That stripped Bobby and Barbara of a possible motive—other than their own bitterness.

Roan thanked him and hung up. Lieutenant Hoberman returned from inside the house carrying a calendar. "Look at this, Deputy Whitefeather. Morty Burns met with his wife's brother Arlis the morning he died."

MEGAN CATALOGED THE details of the crime scene. For some reason the older woman's face had gotten to her. Judging from the pictures on the mantel and bookshelf she was a cookie-baking grandmother who doted on her grandchildren.

It was a senseless death that made Megan determined to find justice for Edith.

"I'm going to notify Arlis Bennett about his sister," Roan said. "If he knows something and is holding back, maybe his sister's murder will be incentive enough for him to talk." He gestured toward Edith as the medics carried her body to the ambulance to transport her to the morgue. "Let me know what you find on the autopsy."

"I will." Megan's phone buzzed as she strode toward her van. "Dr. Lail."

"Dr. Lail, this is Ruth Cumberland. What in the world did you say to my husband to upset him so much? I've never seen him so distraught. I thought he was having a heart attack."

Megan bit her lip. Obviously Dr. Cumberland hadn't revealed her findings. She couldn't disclose the details, either. "I'm sorry he's not feeling well, Mrs. Cumberland. The past few weeks seem to have gotten to him."

A tense moment passed. "There's more to it than that, and I think you're the cause. I realize you're young and think you know everything, but my husband is a good man. So leave him alone."

Megan's pulse hammered at the accusation in the woman's voice.

She opened her mouth to respond, but the phone clicked into silence. Troubled by Mrs. Cumberland's reaction, Megan started her van and left the farm.

Even if she was upsetting people, Megan had a job to do, and she didn't intend to be intimidated. She'd admired the ME who'd pushed to find the truth about her sister's death, and she would push for the truth for the victims who wound up on her table.

Poor Edith's grandchildren would not have the pleasure of growing up with her or spending holidays in her kitchen baking cookies. Someone had to make that right. Or at least as right as it could be.

Her killer had to pay.

By the time she arrived at the morgue, the medics were bringing Edith's body inside. She struggled to remain professional as she prepared to start the autopsy.

Once she had Edith on the table, she took a few moments to talk to her as she often did her patients. "I'm going to find out who did this to you, Edith. I promise." She stroked the woman's gray hair from her face, the brittle strands breaking off as she did. Dried blood and spittle darkened the corners of her lips, her mouth wide-open in a scream for help.

Forcing her emotions at bay, she donned her gear and began the gruesome task of the autopsy, speaking into her mic and entering the details of stomach contents, scars, injuries and forensics as she worked.

Just as she suspected, Edith had bled out from the gunshot wound. She recovered the bullet. It appeared to be from a .45. Morty had been shot by a .45, as well.

Edith also had a scar from a C-section, suffered from rheumatoid arthritis, had her tonsils removed and had last eaten biscuits and gravy.

Megan put time of death as the night before, being the same day her husband died, only Edith had died hours after her husband. So not a murder-suicide.

The bullet suggested they were murdered by the same person. But why kill Morty then his wife? Had she known her husband's killer?

If so, why wouldn't she have gone to the police? Instead, she was home preparing dinner.

Because she hadn't known he was dead.

Megan sent the bullet to the ballistics lab to corroborate her suspicions and informed Lieutenant Hoberman about the time of death.

"We'll look at phone records between the couple and others, and their financials. Hopefully some prints will turn up at the house."

She thanked him and hung up, the image of Edith's ashen, shocked face haunting her as she finished documenting the results.

When she finally checked the clock, it was way past dinnertime. The night shift would be on duty now, the hospital quiet as the patients settled in for the night. Of course the morgue was always quiet, especially since it was housed in the left quadrant of the basement.

She hung her lab coat on the peg on the wall and rubbed a hand over the back of her neck with a tired sigh.

But just as she stepped into the hall leading to the cold room and elevators, the hall lights flickered off. She frowned, feeling her way toward the wall for the light switch, but a noise startled her.

Footsteps.

Then suddenly someone slammed her up against the wall and shoved a knee into her back. Megan grunted and tried to fight.

But her attacker stuck the barrel of a gun against her spine.

It was cold. Hard. The click of a bullet in the chamber rent the air.

She screamed and swung her elbow back to fight,

but he pinned her against the wall and yanked something thick and heavy over her head, pitching her into darkness.

Chapter Seven

Roan studied the Circle T ranch as he knocked on the door. Thanks to the McCullens, the owner, Boyle Gates, was serving time for cattle rustling.

His cousin Arlis Bennett had moved in to run the business while Gates was incarcerated. The bigger question was if Bennett had known about his cousin's illegal activities and had been an accomplice. So far no charges had been brought against the man.

Judging from the size of the herd on the property, Bennett seemed to be maintaining the ranch. The community and local cattlemen's club were watching, though, just in case he resumed Gates's underhanded methods to add to his stock.

Night had set in, the heavy clouds threatening rain. Megan had texted him with news that Edith was shot with a .45, same as her husband.

Footsteps shuffled inside the house, then the door opened. A tall ruddy-faced man in his fifties stood there, Western shirt neatly pressed, his jeans new and stiff.

Roan doubted Bennett lifted a hand on the ranch himself. He probably had his hands do all the dirty work.

Including the men he'd hired to sabotage Horseshoe Creek.

He just needed some proof, dammit.

"Mr. Bennett?"

"Yes."

"I'm Deputy Whitefeather."

"I know who you are. You work with the Mc-Cullens."

"Actually, I work for the people in Pistol Whip."

Bennett held up his hands. "My hands are clean. You can look at my books and see all my stock was bought legitimately."

He was probably smart enough to fake paperwork. "Actually, that's not the reason I'm here. Can I come in?"

Bennett raised a bushy eyebrow. "I guess so."

The burly man stepped aside and gestured for Roan to enter. Roan followed him to a large study with dark wood paneling, a giant cherry desk and credenza complete with a wet bar.

"Drink?" Bennett offered.

Roan shook his head. "I'm on duty. But you can go ahead."

Bennett shot him a dark scowl as if he didn't need anyone's permission. He poured an expensive-looking bourbon into a tumbler, then carried it to a leather chair and took a seat.

Roan claimed the chair opposite him.

"All right, what is this about?"

Roan swallowed hard. He hated this part of the job. "Mr. Bennett, have you talked to your sister lately?"

Bennett's eyes narrowed suspiciously. "Not for a few days. Why?"

Roan folded his hands. "What about her husband, Morty?"

A long sigh. "Two weeks ago. He came begging for money."

"And?"

"Burns was good to my sister, but he didn't know how to manage his land. He also liked to gamble and whittled away their income and savings to the point where they were about to lose their farm."

So he was desperate for money.

"Did you help him out?"

"At first," Bennett admitted. "I talked to Edith. Told her what he'd done. They fought, but she refused to leave him." He shrugged. "I did what I could to help. But finally I had to cut him off."

So Burns might have been desperate enough to take money to do something illegal, like set fire to the barns on Horseshoe Creek.

Bennett sipped his drink. "Now, why are you asking all these questions about Morty and Edith?"

Roan worked his mouth from side to side. "I'm sorry to have to inform you of this, Mr. Bennett, but both Mr. Burns and your sister are dead."

Bennett's eyes widened, then he threw back the rest of his drink. "What happened? How?"

The man's shock seemed genuine. Then again, Roan didn't know him well enough to determine if he was lying.

"They were both murdered. Shot at close range." He cleared his throat. "Mr. Burns's body was found dumped outside Pistol Whip."

Bennett's hand trembled as he clutched the empty glass. "And my sister?"

"She was found in her house."

Bennett pinched the bridge of his nose and blinked as if struggling with his emotions. "When…" his voice cracked "…did it happen?"

"The ME put her death last night." Roan forced a calm to his tone. "Where were you then?"

Anger flared in the man's eyes. "You can't be serious. You think I'd kill my only sister?"

"It's a standard question, Mr. Bennett. Where were you?"

His nostrils flared as he stood. He walked over and poured himself another drink, then turned to face Roan, his eyes seething. "Here on the ranch. My housekeeper can verify that."

"All day and night?"

"Yes."

Roan stood. "One more question, Mr. Bennett. Do you own a .45?"

A muscle ticked in Bennett's jaw. "No."

But a quick flicker of his gaze toward the wall

on the opposite side of the room suggested he was lying. Roan scrutinized the area and noticed a painting of a waterfall.

He'd bet his job that a safe was hidden beneath that painting. And that Bennett had a .45 tucked inside.

Dammit. He needed a warrant to look through it.

Bennett gestured toward the door, indicating he was done with the interview. "Instead of hassling me, why don't you look into the men Morty owed money to. Maybe they killed him and Edith because he couldn't pay his debts."

Roan gave a clipped nod. That was a possibility, although how could someone collect money from a dead man who was broke?

No…he had a bad feeling his suspicions were right, that their murders were connected to the McCullens.

That Bennett was offering an alternative person of interest to steer suspicion from himself.

MEGAN STRUGGLED TO BREATHE, but the thick body bag was suffocating. She couldn't see, couldn't think for the fear threatening to choke her.

God…she didn't want to die.

She kicked her foot backward and managed to connect with her attacker's knee. He grunted in pain, but tightened his hold around her neck. Then he pressed his mouth against her ear through the bag.

"Leave Joe McCullen's death alone or you'll end up in this bag for good."

She tried to pry his fingers from her neck and felt latex gloves. Still, she scratched and clawed, desperate to get skin or at least some fibers to help identify him later. If she survived...

He jerked her forward, then something hard slammed against the back of her head. The next second, the world was spinning. She fought to remain conscious, the darkness swallowing her.

Another blow and she collapsed with a groan. Terrified, she blinked, silently willing herself not to black out, but pain shot through her skull, then a numbness crept over her. Blinding colors...black dots...room swirling...

She couldn't move, couldn't lift her hands, make her legs work. She tried to scream, but her voice was lost as he stuffed her in the body bag. The sound of the zipper rasping echoed as if it was far away, and she had the strange sensation of floating...

She looked down at herself in the bag, and then she was lying naked on the autopsy table...

ROAN DROVE FROM Bennett's to the prison where Boyle Gates was incarcerated, hoping to get some answers. A sliver of a moon tried to claw its way through the storm clouds, occasionally adding a tiny flicker of light to the dark sky. Otherwise the land that stretched between Pistol Whip and the jail seemed desolate.

He phoned Megan to see if she'd found anything helpful with Edith Burns's autopsy, but her voice mail kicked in, so he left a message for her to call him.

Then he punched Lieutenant Hoberman's number. "Did you find anything linking the Burns couple to the fires at Horseshoe Creek?"

"Not directly," Hoberman said. "Although there was a can of gasoline in the toolshed. But a lot of farmers have gasoline cans."

"True." Dammit.

"How about his financials?"

"Bank accounts were slim, although there was a deposit of ten thousand dollars made about a week ago."

"Any idea where it came from?"

"No, it was a cash deposit."

Just as he'd expected. No paper trail.

Although it was past visiting hours, he explained to the warden about the Burnses' murders and that he wanted to see Gates's reaction before anyone had a chance to inform him of the news.

Of course, if he'd paid to have the couple killed, he already knew. He and Bennett could have worked together. Or Bennett could have inadvertently told Gates about his sister's troubles and Gates took advantage and offered to help Burns out of his mess if he did him a favor.

Roan settled into the chair in the visiting room, pasting on a professional face as the guard led Gates into the room. He'd seen the rancher around Pistol Whip with his air of superiority and disliked him immediately. He had also given some of Roan's people hell about some land that they insisted belonged to the res. He wanted to buy it and tried to push them off, but thankfully the law had been on the side of the Native Americans.

Even in his prison uniform, Gates still exuded that cocky attitude. "What do you want, Whitefeather?"

The way he said Roan's name sounded condescending, as if he thought Roan wasn't good enough to share the same space with him.

"I thought you might be ready to talk."

Gates rubbed a hand over his smoothly shaven jaw. "I've already said all I have to say."

"Did you hire Stan Romley to set those fires at Horseshoe Creek?"

Gates's eyes flashed with rage. "No. I already told the sheriff that. And if you think you're going to persuade me to confess to something, you're dead wrong."

"What about Morty Burns? Did you pay him to sabotage the ranch?"

Gates shot up, handcuffs jangling. "This is absurd." He jerked his head toward the guard. "Take me back to my cell."

"Sit down, Gates," Roan said firmly. "I'm not finished."

"Well, I am," Gates said in a tone that brooked no argument.

"No, you're not." Roan jerked his thumb toward the chair, an order to sit down. "Right now I have two bodies in the morgue. Two that I believe you are connected to."

Gates went still, questions flashing across his face. "What bodies?"

Roan thumped his foot for a minute, intentionally making the man wait.

"You came here to talk to me, Whitefeather, so talk. What bodies are you referring to?"

"Morty and Edith Burns."

A brief flicker of Gates's eyes was his only reaction, but it indicated he knew more than he was willing to say. Maybe he'd even known about their deaths.

"What do they have to do with me?"

"The wife, Edith, was Arlis Bennett's sister. I talked to Arlis. He claims that Morty was in financial trouble."

"Again," Gates said, his voice cold. "What does that have to do with me?"

"This is what I think. I think you and your cousin Bennett are working together. You needed someone to do your dirty work, so you hired Romley. Maybe you hired Burns, too. He could have helped with the cattle rustling. Maybe he sabotaged Horseshoe Creek."

"That's ridiculous."

"Is it? The man was desperate to save his farm. Edith was your cousin just like Arlis is, so you offered to bail out her husband. But things went sour. He wanted more money or tried to blackmail you and you had to get rid of him."

"You're forgetting something. I've been in prison for weeks."

Roan stood, his mouth a thin line. "Yes, you have. But you forget—I know how prisons work. How easy it is to hire someone from the inside."

"You really think I'd kill my own cousin?"

"To protect yourself? Yes."

Gates stared at him for a heartbeat then spit. The guard stepped forward to reprimand him, but Roan gestured for him to wait.

"When I get the proof I need, you'll go back to trial, Gates. And this time you won't be eligible for parole. You'll be on death row."

"Wait just a damn minute," Gates said when Roan headed toward the door.

Roan paused and folded his arms. "What?"

"Instead of trying to pin everything on me, why don't you look at the other people who had a grudge against Joe McCullen?"

Roan maintained a neutral expression, although he was hoping for a lead. "And who would that be?"

"Elmore Clark."

"I know about Clark. But McCullen helped Clark out by buying his land, and he kept it for him in case he got back on his feet and wanted it back."

Gates cursed. "That's a bald-faced lie. Joe refused to give Clark water rights and forced Clark to sell. Then McCullen put Clark out on the street. Clark hated the McCullens for years."

MEGAN'S HEAD THROBBED as she slowly opened her eyes, but an empty, black darkness swallowed her.

She fought for a breath, but the air felt hot, sticky, the air stifling. She reached up to find her way from the empty hollowness, but her hand struck something heavy, thick…vinyl. Then something hard above…

Slowly her memory returned, and fear choked her. The man…he'd attacked her. Covered her head with that body bag.

Panic shot through her and she tried to move, but she was trapped inside the body bag. There was no space, no room. The buzzing sound of the fluorescent lights in the morgue echoed above her.

The truth dawned quickly. Oh, God.

She was locked in one of the drawers in the cold room where they stored the corpses.

Terrified, she started to scream…

Chapter Eight

Roan checked his watch. Too late to talk to Clark tonight. He'd catch up with him first thing in the morning.

Megan still hadn't returned his call, so he punched her number again. The phone rang three, four times, but her voice mail kicked in again. Dammit. Where was she?

Still working on the autopsy?

Knowing her, she wouldn't leave until she'd processed each and every detail of the body and then she'd look for more. He liked the fact that she was meticulous in her job, dedicated and that she took great pains with the bodies that ended up on her table. She had more compassion for the dead than most people did for the living.

But…earlier she'd thought someone had pushed her into the street… What if her questions about this case—or another one she'd worked on—had upset someone enough to want her to stop nosing around?

Anxiety knotted his shoulders as he left the prison and drove back to Pistol Whip. The storm clouds that had threatened earlier opened up and raindrops splattered the windshield. They'd had a dry spell lately, and the farms and ranches needed this rain, but it reminded him too much of the night his mother died.

He'd held her while she'd passed, the rain battering the hogan where they lived in an erratic rhythm that had mirrored his pounding heart. He'd felt so helpless. Had wanted to do something to save her.

But nothing, not his prayers or the chants of the medicine man, not even the modern medicine Dr. Cumberland had brought, had been enough.

He blinked back emotions, but the pain was just as raw as it had been then. Only Megan had stood by him, offering soft soothing words and her comforting arms.

And he'd taken advantage. He'd needed her so damn much that even as he ordered himself to walk away, he hadn't had the strength.

Hell, why was he thinking about her now? Especially in that way…

She was helping him with a case—that's all there could be between them.

Deciding to fill her in on his conversations with Bennett and Gates, he drove by her house, hoping she was home. But her van wasn't in the drive.

She had to be at the morgue.

He spun the car around and headed toward the hospital. Maybe Megan had discovered something concrete that would tie Bennett or Gates to Edith Burns's murder.

MEGAN FOUGHT PANIC. She was trapped in a body bag inside one of the drawers in the cold room.

But she was alive.

At least for now.

She tried to slow her breathing to preserve oxygen. How long could she survive in here? The temperature was meant to keep the bodies from decomposing further before she could complete the autopsy. Even after she finished, the bodies were tagged and preserved before transporting to the funeral home or cremation center.

At this temperature, she might develop hypothermia, but she could recover from that if someone found her in time.

In the morning, Howard would show up for work. Or Dr. Cumberland might stop by.

In spite of her logic and rationale, tears filled her eyes. What if one of them didn't come in? If they didn't have a new case, Howard might just go straight to the lab. There he would discover the results of her findings on Edith for him to process.

Unless he had questions for her, he'd likely spend the morning analyzing the samples and data she'd collected.

God…she could be here all night, and by morning she'd be too weak to cry out for help.

Cold terror engulfed her, making her tremble.

A sob rose in her throat, her pulse clamoring. She was claustrophobic.

Always had been.

She didn't like elevators or small spaces. Even as a child, she'd had a panic attack on the submarine ride at the water park.

She struggled to move her hands and arms and managed to feel in her pocket. If she had a scalpel or sharp pen inside, she could rip the bag. But…her pocket was empty. She'd left all her tools on the tray when she'd finished.

In spite of the cold, sweat pooled on her body, soaking her clothes and lab coat. A sob escaped her, and even as she reminded herself to breathe slowly, she struggled for air. Short panting breaths ripped from her lungs and nausea clogged her throat.

She gagged, fighting the urge to throw up. That would only make her situation worse.

Desperate to escape, she used her fingernails to tear at the bag, but her short nails didn't break the surface. Still, she tried to rip the material. When that failed, she pinched together a portion of it and tried to tear it with both hands.

Her hands shook, frustration clawing at her. It was no use. The material was too thick and strong…

Tears mingled with the sweat now, running down her face, into her mouth and down her neck.

She thought she heard a noise from somewhere in the building. Maybe Howard had come back for some reason. Or maybe Dr. Cumberland.

She held her breath and listened, but the sound was an ambulance…

Frantic, she raised her fists and beat against the top of the drawer, then used her feet to pound the bottom.

ROAN PHONED MEGAN AGAIN, but once again received her voice mail.

Worry kicked in.

Something was wrong. She would have answered or returned his calls by now.

The last time they'd talked, she was headed to the hospital to perform the autopsy on Edith Burns. She might still be there.

Unless something had happened to her.

Vehicles slowed because of the rain, and he veered around them. A truck raced toward him, lights nearly blinding him, and he flashed his lights to warn the driver to watch it.

Rain spewed from the road onto his windshield as the truck flew past. He cursed, flipped his wipers to full speed and turned onto the side street leading to the hospital. He drove through the doctors' parking lot and found Megan's van.

Lights from an ambulance blinked and twirled by the entrance to the ER and a car screeched to a stop behind it. A young couple jumped out just as the medics unloaded an elderly man from the back. They raced in, obviously upset.

He understood the panic. If anything had happened to Megan, he didn't know what he'd do. He should have insisted she give him the results then stay out of the investigation.

He threw his car into Park in one of the visitor spaces, then jogged through the rain to the hospital entrance. He shook off the rainwater as he stepped inside, then hurried to the elevator.

He jumped inside, hoping he was panicking for nothing. That Megan had just gotten caught up in work or silenced her phone.

The doors dinged open. The basement lighting was dim, the halls virtually empty. His footsteps echoed on the floor as he rushed toward the morgue.

The empty dark halls echoed with the dead, the scents of chemicals and antiseptics permeating the walls in an attempt to cover the fact that this place was where the deceased went as a midway stop to their final resting place.

He tried the door but it was locked and the lights were off. Dammit, Megan's car was outside. If she wasn't here, where was she?

Maybe she met up with someone. Maybe she had a date.

The thought irritated him, although he had no idea why. Besides, Megan was in the middle of an autopsy tonight. He couldn't imagine her leaving Edith's body and the questions about her murder to go out for a frivolous evening.

Then again, he could be projecting himself onto

her. But… Megan had depth. She was here. He felt it in his gut.

He banged on the door, then peered through the glass partition, but it was hard to see through the blinds, especially with the lights off.

"Megan!" He knocked again, then tapped on the glass. The sound of the glass rattling and his own voice reverberated off the walls. He paused, listening for signs of anyone inside, but heard nothing.

"Megan," he tried again. "If you're here, let me in. We need to talk."

Another hesitation. Seconds ticked by. His heart began to race. His shoulders tightened.

She was in there. He felt it. She needed help.

He sensed it just as he'd sensed when his mother was dying and needed him to come to her side that night.

Fear wrapped his heart in a choke hold. No, this was nothing like that.

Except he couldn't leave until he was certain Megan was safe. What if she was hurt? Injured? Too helpless to call out?

Adrenaline surged through him and he picked the door lock. The door squeaked open and he stepped inside, senses alert for the sound of a voice or breathing. Anything to indicate that someone was there.

The strong scent of formaldehyde assaulted him as he strode through the office and into the autopsy room. The metal trays and pans appeared clean, the gurneys empty, the table and floor hosed down.

Megan had finished the autopsy on Edith Burns and would have then returned her to the cold room. Pulse hammering, he walked through the room and checked the door to the hallway.

The furnace rumbled. Air whistled through the vents, and the fluorescent lights buzzed as he flipped on the light switch. Bright light illuminated the hall, accentuating the walls stained with dirt and the scent of death. No matter how hard they tried, it couldn't be eliminated or erased.

Fear gripped him as he stepped toward the cold room. Edith's body was stored in there, along with whomever else the morgue had received. It was dark. Locked. No sounds from inside.

Again, though, icy fear traipsed up his spine as if the dead had whispered his name, begging for help.

Ridiculous. He did not believe in hocus-pocus, although he had been raised to trust the shaman on the res.

"Megan!" he shouted. "If you're in here, somewhere, show me a damn sign."

He gripped the door handle, heart hammering, breath trapped in his chest. Silence. The rattling of the building. Rain outside.

Then another sound. Something soft. Muffled. Then a bang.

Was it from inside?

It couldn't be. But…he pressed his ear to the door

and listened again. Another muffled sound. Another bang.

Panic shot through him, and he gripped the door and tried to yank it open. It didn't budge. He cursed, quickly picked the lock on that door. He shoved it open with a growl, then flipped on a light and noted the bank of body drawers.

Dear God, was she inside one of those?

MEGAN FOUGHT TEARS and blind panic as she kicked at the drawer and screamed. Her cries came out low and throaty, her voice weak from repeatedly yelling for help. Her lungs ached for air and sweat poured down her face and body, yet she shivered with cold fear.

Had she heard someone outside? A footstep? A voice?

"Help!" she cried. "Please help me." She sucked in a breath, pulled her legs back as far as she could in the small space, then used every ounce of her energy to slam both feet against the bottom of the drawer. At the same time, she pounded the top of the box, but the body bag muffled the sound so much she wasn't sure anyone could hear it from the outside.

Tears trickled down her cheeks as she called out for help again and again. If she escaped, she'd make certain the medical examiner's office installed latches to open the drawers from the inside in case someone were to get trapped again.

Another kick. Another cry. Another pounding of her fist.

Her arms were growing weak. Her voice cracking. Low. Hardly discernible to her own ears. Her feet barely connected with the last kick.

Exhausted, she sagged inside the bag, the heavy plastic clinging to her damp skin, her body weak. She couldn't hold out much longer.

Despair filled her. She was going to die in here and no one would find her until it was too late…

Chapter Nine

Roan stared at the rows of drawers, his stomach knotting. One thing he'd learned on the res was to respect the dead.

But if Megan was in there, he had to look.

He rolled his hands into fists, listening again. Had he heard a noise or was it simply the sound of the rain beating against the building?

A low sound then…barely discernible. A…cry?

Pulse hammering, he crossed the room. Praying he didn't find Megan dead, he jerked open the first drawer, but it was empty. The second one held Edith Burns's body.

"I'm sorry, ma'am," he said in a low voice as he closed her back up.

Suddenly a noise broke through the quiet. Another bang.

He stiffened and hurried to the last drawer where the sound had come from. Hand shaking, he pulled the drawer open. A body bag held someone…there was movement…

"Megan?"

A cry rent the air.

"Megan!" Dear God.

He yanked at the zipper, but it was stuck, so he jerked on it again. Finally the tab gave way and he shoved down the zipper. Megan lay inside, pale and gasping for a breath.

"I'm here, baby." He pulled the drawer the rest of the way open and grabbed her beneath the shoulders. She was fighting, pushing at the body bag, trembling.

"I've got you," he said against her neck as he shoved at the bag and dragged her from the drawer. She struggled to get out of the suffocating vinyl and he yanked it away, then she sagged into his arms. He carried her from the cold room through the autopsy room to her office, his emotions pinging all over the place.

She was crying, her body shaking as she clung to him. He sank onto the small love seat in her office and held her in his lap, pressing her face into his chest and rocking her back and forth.

"You're okay, Megan, I've got you."

He cradled her against him, soothing her and stroking her until she finally calmed and her tears subsided. Slowly her breathing steadied, and he felt her relaxing, felt the panic seep from her.

Dammit, how long had she been in that drawer? And who the hell had put her there?

MEGAN HATED ANY WEAKNESS, but she couldn't stop herself from trembling. It was a natural reaction

to the cold and trauma, the scientist in her reminded herself.

But it was more than that and she knew it. She'd
been terrified of dying inside one of the very drawers where she stored the corpses she autopsied.

"Megan?"

Roan's husky voice drifted through the fog of
fear enveloping her.

"Do you need me to call a medic?"

She shook her head against his chest, still struggling to gather her composure.

He gently brushed her tear-soaked hair from her
cheek. "Are you sure? If you need a doctor, just
say so."

"I'm…okay," she said, her voice barely a whisper.

His chest rose and fell with his breath, a comforting feeling as she soaked up his strength and the
body heat emanating from him. She didn't know if
she'd ever get warm again.

He cradled her closer, then lifted her chin with
his thumb and forced her to look at him. "You'd tell
me if you're hurt?"

Her teeth chattered, but she gave a slight nod.
"I'm just s-so cold."

A muscle ticked in his jaw. His eyes were dark
with anger. "How long were you in there?"

"I don't know," she said. "It seemed like forever."

His mouth softened slightly. "What happened?"

A shudder coursed through her, and she closed

her eyes and buried her head against him. "Someone attacked me."

His body tensed, but he continued soothing her with a gentle stroke of his hand along her arm. "Did you see who it was?"

She shook her head again. "He came up behind me…and he shoved the bag over my face… I tried to fight, but he hit me in the back of my head."

Roan lifted her slightly and angled her head to examine her. "Dammit, you are hurt. You have a knot the size of a golf ball."

"I tried not to pass out," she said in a pained voice. "Then he shoved me in that body bag. I tried to fight him, but…he hit me again, and I blacked out."

"Bastard." He stroked her arms to warm her. "You need to be examined. You might have a concussion."

"I don't want a doctor," Megan said, another chill washing over her. "I just want to go home and take a shower."

"We have to get a team here to see if he left prints."

"He didn't," Megan said. "I tried to scratch him, but he was wearing gloves."

"Still, maybe you snagged a button or something."

"Maybe." She doubted it, but he was right. If there was a chance her attacker had left any piece of evidence behind, it might help catch him.

And she wanted the son of a bitch caught.

Roan captured her face between his hands and looked into her eyes. Worry furrowed his brows, but he looked so handsome and strong that she lost herself in his dark eyes.

"Hang in there, Megan, I'll call a crime team."

She agreed, although when Roan helped her into the chair and stood to make the call, she missed his warm arms around her.

ROAN PHONED LIEUTENANT HOBERMAN and explained the circumstances. "Thanks. We'll wait here."

When he ended the call, Megan stood on wobbly legs and smoothed her hair back into her bun with her fingers. He wanted to tell her to leave it down, that even shaken and upset she looked beautiful. But he realized she needed to regain control, and part of that was putting herself back together.

"I'm going to the ladies' room."

"Megan, wait. Maybe you shouldn't wash your hands yet, just in case you got some forensics under your nails."

She hesitated, eyes flickering with unease, then acceptance. "You're right." She folded her arms across her chest and straightened her spine. "I wasn't thinking."

Compassion for her filled him, and he stroked her cheek with his thumb. "It's all right. You just went through a terrible ordeal."

Her lower lip quivered, but she clamped her teeth

over it as if to calm herself. "I can't believe this." She gestured around her office. "Odd, but I always felt safe here. Now…"

"Your job means you encounter death, Megan. That's not pretty. And you have had three murder victims on your table this week."

"That's true." She paced across the room. "Roan, the man who attacked me told me to leave Joe Mc-Cullen's death alone."

Roan's heart jumped. "He said that?"

She nodded, her face paling again. "He said if I didn't leave it alone, I'd end up in that body bag permanently."

Roan cursed. The bastard had threatened Megan's life. He knotted his hands into fists. If he got ahold of him, he'd kill him.

His phone buzzed with a text. Hoberman and his team had arrived.

The next hour the crime team investigators combed the morgue, Megan's office and the cold room searching for anything Megan's assailant might have left behind. They bagged the body bag to take to the lab and scraped beneath Megan's nails.

She resorted to professional mode, answering questions as if the attack had happened to a stranger.

"We found a hair," one of the techs said. "Short, dark."

"It's not mine," Megan said, stating the obvious.

"Could it belong to one of the bodies you have here?" Lieutenant Hoberman asked.

She chewed the inside of her cheek. "I don't think so. But I'll collect a sample from each one for comparison."

Roan admired her strength, and realized taking action was a coping mechanism. He also watched to make sure she hadn't dismissed the blow to her head too quickly, that she hadn't sustained a concussion.

One reason he intended to stay the night with her.

The other…he needed to know that she was alive, and that the man who'd attacked her didn't return to her house to make good on that threat.

MEGAN REPLAYED THE past few hours in her head as the crime team processed the lab. She gathered samples of the hair on the bodies in the morgue, but judging from texture, color and length, none of them were a match.

Maybe her attacker had left a strand of his hair. Hair held DNA.

Whether the person it belonged to would be in the system was the question. If not they'd have to find a suspect to compare it to.

"Who else has been in the morgue and your office?" Roan asked.

Megan massaged her temple with two fingers. "Me. Dr. Cumberland. Howard, my lab analyst. There are a couple of other techs and the chief ME, although he doesn't come in regularly anymore."

"We need all their names and DNA samples," Roan said.

"I'll make a list. Their DNA should be on file."

"Right. Can you think of anyone else? A family member or friend who came in to make an identification?"

Megan searched her memory banks. "The wife of a car accident victim, but she was in her seventies with gray hair."

Roan claimed the seat across from her. "Megan, did you talk to anyone else about Joe McCullen's autopsy?"

She shook her head no. "Just Dr. Cumberland. He was so distraught he left the office. And of course Howard, the tech who ran the tests, knew."

"You trust him to be discreet?"

"Yes. Explicitly. Besides, he didn't even know the McCullens. Why would he want to hurt any of them?"

"He may not have. But he could have talked to the wrong person without realizing it."

"I know Howard, Roan. I'm telling you he would never discuss a case outside the office. That is, unless it was with me."

Roan seemed to consider her statement. "You said Dr. Cumberland was distraught?"

"Yes. His wife called me, upset. She said she'd never seen her husband so emotional." Megan hesitated, still disturbed by the conversation with the woman. "I think she was afraid I was going to try to ruin Dr. Cumberland's reputation by exposing that he'd made a mistake. He's supposed to retire this year."

"But you didn't mention doing that?"

"Of course not. I'm sure he didn't realize what was happening to Joe. He loved Joe and his sons. He cried like a baby at Joe's funeral."

"Have you had trouble with anyone else lately?"

Megan thought back to the man at the bar and relayed what had happened. "But he has nothing to do with Joe McCullen."

"True. But he could have shot at you in the street."

Megan shivered. "Or the person who fired that shot could have been trying to scare me, and it could be the same man who attacked me."

Roan squeezed her hand. "We will get to the bottom of this, Megan. Meanwhile don't discuss this case with anyone. I haven't told Maddox or his brothers yet. They deserve to know first."

"I agree. And, Roan, I would never discuss medical findings with anyone not involved or authorized in the case. I took an oath."

"I'm not questioning you," Roan said in a husky voice that touched something deep inside her. "I just don't want to see you get hurt. Obviously our investigation is making someone nervous."

The crime team finished and Lieutenant Hoberman told Roan he'd call him with the results of his findings. Megan stood, anxious to leave.

"Thanks for coming, Roan. I appreciate all you did."

He rubbed her arm, his dark eyes intense. "I'll follow you home, Megan."

Relief filled her. She didn't want to act like a simpering female, but flashbacks of nearly suffocating taunted her. "Thanks."

He nodded and she locked up, then they walked to her car. "I'm right behind you," Roan said. "When you get to your house, don't go inside. I want to search it first."

The idea that someone might be waiting for her at home sent another streak of terror through Megan.

She didn't want to be alone tonight. But how could she ask Roan to stay without making him think that she wanted to be with him again?

You do want to be with him.

Yes, she did. But she'd been raised to be tough and strong. After all, she didn't have her looks to fall back on. She'd have to remember that when Roan was at her house.

Although, as she closed her door and started the engine, she could still feel that man's breath on her neck. His hands nearly choking her.

She could hear the sound of the zipper rasping as he closed her inside that body bag. She could feel darkness choking her when she'd awakened, locked in that drawer...

His menacing warning reverberated in her ears. Had she heard that voice before?

Chapter Ten

Tension thrummed inside Roan as he followed Megan back to her house. He kept his eyes peeled in case someone was following her, but the truck that fell in behind her as she turned through town eventually veered into the parking lot for The Silver Bullet.

He replayed the scene Megan had described in his head a half-dozen times, his anger mounting. If whoever had attacked her saw her with him, would he assume she'd talked? Would he come after her again?

Hell, he was damned if he did and damned if he didn't. Because there was no way he'd leave her alone now.

This son of a bitch wouldn't get away with terrorizing her. And if he'd killed Joe—his father—he had to go to jail.

He had to tell Maddox—soon.

Speaking of Maddox, his phone buzzed and the man's name appeared. Had he heard what had happened?

"Deputy Whitefeather."

"It's Maddox."

"Did you get Romley?"

"No, he escaped. But I'm on his trail now. He hooked up with a woman named Darcy at a bar. She said he told her he's headed west. I'll keep you posted. Anything going on there?"

Roan hated to lie to his boss. But how could he tell Maddox he was his half brother and that their father had been murdered on the phone? That was a conversation to be had in person.

"I'm taking care of things," he said instead.

Maddox thanked him. "Hopefully I'll have Romley in custody by tomorrow and be able to head home."

Twenty-four hours. He needed every second.

Maddox disconnected, and Roan turned into Megan's driveway and parked behind her. The rain had stopped, but the dark clouds still shaded the moon, pitching her yard and house into darkness.

He scanned the perimeter and pulled out his weapon as he climbed from his car. Megan opened her door and slid out. Her face still looked pale, her face gaunt.

"Stay here until I search the house."

She touched his arm. "Be careful, Roan."

He shrugged off her concern. "Just doing my job." Except protecting Megan felt more personal. That one night they'd shared had made it that way.

An animal howled from the woods behind her house, and somewhere nearby a dog barked. She handed him the keys, and he gripped them in his free hand, his other hand tightening around his gun.

The steps creaked as he eased up them. He paused to listen at the door before he opened it. Everything seemed quiet.

Although he doubted Megan's attacker would strike twice in the same night, someone could be lurking inside.

He eased open the door, pausing again, but the entryway was quiet and so was the rest of the house. He used his pocket flashlight to illuminate the area, then inched into the den, then the attached kitchen. Everything appeared in order.

He eased into the hall and checked the bedrooms. Once again quiet. Nothing out of place.

Relieved, he hurried back through the house to tell Megan. He motioned that it was okay for her to come in, then waited as she climbed the steps.

"The house is clean," Roan said.

"I'm going to take a shower," Megan said. "Thanks for following me home."

He cleared his throat, hating the fear lingering in her voice. "I'm staying here, Megan. Just in case."

Her gaze met his, relief, then some other emotion he couldn't quite define, flickering in her eyes.

He couldn't erase what had happened to her earlier. But he could protect her tonight.

MEGAN BREATHED A sigh of relief that Roan had insisted on staying with her. She detested showing fear or appearing weak, but she also was no martyr. Realistically the man who'd threatened her could be watching her. If he saw Roan, would he assume she'd told him everything? That she wouldn't give up her questions as he'd demanded?

"If you're hungry, there's some homemade soup in the fridge."

Roan raised a brow. "You cook?"

Megan shrugged. "I had to. My mom was too busy with my sister and her beauty pageants to do it."

She realized she sounded bitter and hadn't meant to.

"I'm sorry, that didn't come out right." She'd told Roan about her sister's murder the night his mother died. Another way they'd bonded. "I loved Shelly."

"I know you did," he said in a gruff tone. "But it sounds like you were the caretaker in the family."

Megan shrugged again. "Obviously I didn't do a very good job or my sister would still be alive."

"Don't do that," Roan said, his voice harder. "Your sister's death wasn't your fault."

Emotions welled in her throat, threatening to send her into another sobbing fit. Determined not to fall apart, she turned away and headed toward the bedroom. "I'll heat up the soup after I shower."

She didn't bother to wait for a response. She shut the bedroom door and sagged against it.

But the smell of the morgue and her own fear was wearing on her. She felt vulnerable and weak, like she might throw herself at Roan if she didn't put some distance between them.

Her phone buzzed as she dropped her purse on the chair in the corner. She checked the caller ID— her father.

He probably just wanted to try to convince her to leave the ME's office again like he had the last time they'd spoken. But she'd been adamant that she liked her job, and she didn't intend to follow the career path he'd mapped out for her.

Worse, if he knew her job had endangered her life, he would insist she leave it.

No matter what she did, she couldn't please him.

She let her voice mail pick up and stripped her clothes, anxious to get rid of the sweat-soaked garments. The warm spray of water felt heavenly, but when she closed her eyes to rinse her hair, a chilling fear shot through her.

Thank God Roan had come looking for her tonight, that he hadn't waited until morning.

She soaped and scrubbed her body and hair, desperate to cleanse herself of the stench of her attacker's hands and the smell of the body bag. His voice reverberated in her ears again, and she shook herself, determined to block out the sound.

Finally the water turned cold, and she dried off and pulled on a pair of jeans and a loose long-sleeved T-shirt. She towel-dried her hair, then combed it and left it to dry on its own. She didn't care tonight if it was an unruly mass of curls.

By the time she entered the kitchen, the smell of coffee and the vegetable soup wafted toward her. The warm homey smells helped her relax.

"I hope it was okay that I went ahead and heated up the soup."

"It's great. Thank you, Roan."

Roan gestured to the table and she sank into a chair. His dark gaze met hers, something hot and sensual simmering between them. He looked so big and handsome in her kitchen that for a moment, she imagined waking up to him every day.

"Megan, I know you've been through a lot tonight, but can you tell me anything else about the man who attacked you? Did his voice sound familiar? Did he have a certain smell? Cigarettes maybe?"

The sexual tension she'd felt humming between them had all been in her mind. Roan was here to do a job.

He would protect her, but she couldn't give him her heart. Men didn't want boring plain Janes like her. They wanted beautiful, flirty, fun women, and that was something she would never be.

ROAN FORCED HIMSELF to keep his mind on the case as he and Megan ate dinner.

Her silence concerned him.

Was she reliving the nightmare of what had happened?

Her phone buzzed again, and she glanced at it, then flipped it to silent.

"You aren't going to answer?"

She shook her head. "It's my father."

Roan sipped his coffee. "Why don't you want to talk to him?"

Megan sighed and set her spoon down. "Because he'll want to know what I'm doing and if I tell him, he'll use it as an excuse to lecture me again on why I should leave the ME's office. He thinks it's a waste of my talent to work on dead people when I could be saving lives."

Roan frowned. "He should be proud of you. You're intelligent, you help families find closure by giving them details about how their loved ones died." His throat grew thick. "And you're compassionate to both the dead and the living."

"That's exactly how I feel about the families," Megan said softly. "I wish my father could understand that."

"Maybe one day he will."

She shrugged as if she doubted it, then ran a hand through the damp strands of her hair. They hung loosely around her shoulders, making her look young and impossibly sexy.

Dammit, he wanted to run his hands through the luscious strands.

"So your father is a doctor?"

She nodded. "A neurosurgeon."

If he was unimpressed with Megan's work, he sure as hell would look down on a half-breed deputy sheriff. After all, what did he have to offer a beautiful, smart woman like Megan?

"Let me guess, he wanted you to follow in his footsteps," he said instead.

Megan looked down at her fingers and nodded. "When my sister died, it tore his heart open," she said softly. "Shelly was so pretty and full of life. He used to light up when she walked into the room. She had him wrapped around her little finger just like my mother did."

"I'm sure he loved you, too."

A sardonic laugh escaped her. "Standing beside Shelly was like putting a cactus next to a sunflower."

Roan didn't like the comparison. "He favored your sister?"

"I couldn't blame him," she said with not even a hint of bitterness. "She was so full of life…her outgoing personality drew everyone to her." The sadness in her expression made his gut churn.

"You would have liked her, Roan. Everyone liked Shelly."

"I like you," he said bluntly. "Stop cutting yourself down and comparing yourself to her, Megan."

Megan's lips parted. "I can't help it. My father—"

"Your father should have appreciated you." He couldn't help himself. He reached across the table and captured her hand in his. Her skin felt cold, her fingers tense in his.

"You are not a cactus," he said in a husky tone.

As Megan stared at their joined hands, tears filled her eyes. "Roan, that's nice of you to say—"

"Shut up." He shoved his chair back and stood, then circled the table and pulled her against him. "I'm not the kind of man who doles out compliments just to do so," he said. "When I say something, I mean it." He cupped her face between his hands. "You are not a cactus."

A slow smile curved her mouth. Damn, she was the most beautiful woman he'd ever seen. And the most humble.

Unable to resist the heat simmering between them, he angled his head and slowly lowered his mouth to hers.

It was a mistake.

It was heaven in a kiss.

He told himself to stop. But he didn't listen.

He'd wanted to kiss her again ever since she'd walked back into his life. He'd never forgotten how sweet and erotic she tasted. How her shy touches made him feel strong and virile.

How her silent surrender made him ache for more.

MEGAN SANK INTO the kiss. Roan's lips felt strong and persuasive, offering her pleasure and a reprieve from everything that had happened.

Still shaky from her ordeal, she gripped his arms to keep herself steady, her heart pounding as he rubbed slow circles on her back. His big hard body felt like an anchor against the tirade of emotions overwhelming her, and she savored his calm, tender kiss.

Tender but erotic.

He teased her lips apart with his tongue, and she parted them on a sigh, need and hunger spiraling through her. She slid her hand up his back, urging him closer, desperate to feel the hard planes of his body against her aching one.

He deepened the kiss, his tongue exploring, his chest rising and falling with a labored breath. Desire heated the air between them as he finally ended the kiss, but he didn't pull away. Instead he trailed kisses along her jaw and neck, nibbling at her ear, then lower to the soft swell of her breasts. She arched her head back on a moan and wished she'd dressed in something sexier after her shower, something easy to strip, like her robe.

She wanted him naked and inside her.

He made a low, throaty sound of appreciation, then slipped one hand over her breast and stroked her. Her nipple beaded, begging for more, and he slid his hand beneath her shirt and cupped her through the lacy barrier of her bra.

One stroke, two, he thumbed one nipple then the other, until warmth pooled in her belly. She ran her hands down his back to his butt and cupped his hips, pleasure stealing through her as he thrust his sex against her heat.

A second later, he reached for her shirt to strip it, but his phone trilled, cutting into the moment.

"Ignore it," she whispered.

For a brief second he did. He kissed her again, more urgently this time, the air charged with their breathing. But it continued to trill, and he gave her an apologetic look, then pulled away.

Megan wrapped her arms around herself, trembling with desire as he snatched the phone from the table.

ROAN WANTED TO pound something in frustration. He wanted to kiss Megan. Take her to bed. Make love to her.

Which was a bad idea.

And now the phone. Bad timing or good?

He checked the number. The McCullens' ranch. He quickly punched Connect.

"Deputy Whitefeather."

"Deputy, it's Rose McCullen." Her voice cracked as if she was crying.

"What's wrong, Rose?"

"It's Maddox," she cried. "He caught Stan Romley, but Maddox was shot. The medics just called and they're on the way with him to the hospital."

"Was he in Cheyenne?"

"No, he tracked Romley back near here. They're taking Maddox to the hospital in town."

Roan froze, stomach churning. "How is he?"

"I don't know," she said brokenly. "He's in critical condition."

Roan clenched the phone with a white-knuckled grip. "I'll meet you at the hospital. Unless you need me to drive you."

"No, Mama Mary and I are going together. We'll see you there."

Roan closed his eyes and said a silent prayer that Maddox would survive.

Chapter Eleven

Megan straightened her clothing, disappointed her interlude with Roan was over. But something was wrong.

The worried expression on Roan's face when he faced her confirmed her fear.

"Who was that?"

"Maddox's wife. Maddox was shot apprehending Romley." Roan pocketed his phone, retrieved his gun from the counter where he'd put it and yanked his keys from his pocket.

"Oh, my God, Roan, is he okay?"

"He's in critical condition. They're transporting him to the hospital." He headed toward the door. "I have to go."

"Wait, I'll go with you."

Roan hesitated. "You don't have to do that, Megan. Get some sleep."

She rubbed her arms, a chill going through her. "I don't think I can sleep, not after what happened tonight."

Roan's dark brows drew together. "All right. But I might be there awhile."

Megan grabbed a jacket and her purse. "That's fine. Maybe I can do something to help."

She didn't know why, but Roan seemed upset. At least she could be there for him. He must be closer to Maddox than she'd realized.

She locked the door as they left and followed him to his car. Roan flipped on the siren as he pulled away and sped toward the hospital.

Anxiety gnawed at Roan as he drove. What if Maddox didn't make it?

He hadn't even divulged to him that his father had been murdered. Maddox deserved to know the truth…

And the truth about you?

Did the brothers deserve to know that, or would telling them they were related to Roan rock their world even more?

In spite of the late hour, a few car lights flickered along the highway, and the clouds opened up and dumped more rain on the ground. He flipped his wipers on, the sound of the rain drumming on the car mirroring the racing of his heart.

Megan remained silent. She was probably exhausted, but obviously didn't want to be alone after her earlier attack.

He maneuvered around a truck creeping along, then another car, water spewing from his tires as he turned into the hospital. He threw the car into Park in the ER parking lot and reached for an umbrella for Megan. She accepted it while he tugged on his jacket and pulled on a Stetson.

Together they slogged through the rain and fog to the hospital door. He spotted Rose and Mama Mary as they entered.

"They just took him back." Rose's voice cracked. "They're prepping him for surgery."

Mama Mary wiped at the tears streaming down her face. "He has to be okay, Miss Rose, he has to be."

Rose looked stricken with fear, but she clutched Mama Mary's hands and squeezed them. "He will be. He's strong."

"I'm Megan Lail, Dr. Lail," Megan said. "Where was he shot?"

"The chest," Rose said. "They think the bullet missed his heart, but it may have struck other vital organs."

Megan put her arm around the woman to console her. "Let me get you and Mama Mary some coffee. Surgery will take a while."

A nurse appeared and greeted Rose. "If you want to see him before surgery, you can come back now."

"I'd like to speak to him, too," Roan said.

The nurse narrowed her eyes. "Are you family?"

Roan itched to reply yes. He was Maddox's half brother. But this was not the way he wanted it to come out. "I'm the deputy sheriff. I need to question him about the shooting."

The nurse glanced at Rose for consent, and she gave a quick nod. Then he and Rose followed the nurse through the ER doors to Maddox.

MEGAN RUSHED TO get coffee for everyone. Roan seemed upset—more than she would have thought.

Although, he worked with Maddox and probably considered him a close friend.

When she made it back to the waiting room, Mama Mary was on the phone talking in a hushed voice. "No, Ray, honey, don't cut your honeymoon short. Rose is with Maddox now, and they're taking him to surgery. I'll call you as soon as he gets out."

The older woman sniffed, then dabbed at her eyes with a tissue. "Yes, I already talked to Brett. I assured him I'd call if I thought you two needed to come home."

Megan stood to the side to offer the woman some privacy. The McCullens had the kind of bond that Megan had always wanted in a family.

Mama Mary disconnected and sank into one of the chairs with a pained sigh. Sympathy welled inside Megan. She carried the tray of coffee to her and offered her one.

"Thank you so much, dear," Mama Mary said.

Megan patted the woman's shoulder. "He'll make it through, Maddox seems strong."

Mama Mary gave a little nod, although fear tightened the lines around her big brown eyes. "I thought that about Mr. Joe, thought nothing would ever get him down, but then he took sick." She wiped at her eyes again. "That was hell, watching that big strong man go downhill. Mr. Joe was a proud man. Lordy, how he loved his boys and his land."

"I understand the brothers lost their mother when they were young, and that you raised them."

Affection for the family was obvious in the sad smile that curved her mouth. "That was a rough time when Ms. Grace died. Mr. Joe was all torn up, and those boys…there was a big hole in their lives."

"She died in a car accident?" Megan asked.

Mama Mary nodded. "Ms. Grace, she was a lovely one, but she had her troubles."

"What kind of troubles?"

"That was between her and Mr. Joe."

Megan sensed there was a lot more to the story. "You mean Barbara and Bobby?"

Mama Mary clasped the coffee and took a long slow sip. "I reckon everyone knows about them now. I surely didn't condone what Joe did, having an affair with that woman, but Ms. Grace was so depressed. They were both struggling."

"If you don't mind me asking, what caused her depression?"

Mama Mary's gaze met hers. "I'm not gossiping about that family. I love them and they've been good to me."

"I'm sorry, I didn't mean to pry," Megan said. "And I certainly would never gossip."

Mama Mary searched her face for a moment then seemed to realize she was sincere. "I just told the boys about this a few days ago. Ms. Grace was pregnant with twins but she lost those babies. She and Mr. Joe were both devastated. And Ms. Grace, her hormones were all out of whack."

"I'm sorry, that must have been terrible. Was she being treated for her depression?" Megan asked.

"Of course. Dr. Cumberland did everything he could for her. But some things are just too hard to come back from."

Megan frowned. "I understand how devastating losing a child can be." Her mother had never gotten over losing Shelly.

Mama Mary squeezed her hand, her gaze sympathetic. "You lost someone, too?"

"My sister. My mother committed suicide later. She couldn't stand to go on without her."

"That's tragic," Mama Mary said. "I'm sure you felt alone and abandoned yourself."

Tears clogged Megan's throat. "I'm sorry, I didn't mean to make this about me. We should be saying a prayer for Maddox."

Mama Mary nodded and closed her eyes to pray.

Megan was so moved by the woman's compassion that she did the same. But her mind kept trying to piece together what had happened to the McCullens.

Both Mr. and Mrs. McCullen had ended up dead. The wife from a car accident.

And Joe…

What would Mama Mary say if she knew that Joe hadn't died of natural causes, that he'd been murdered?

ROAN STOOD BACK and gave Rose a few moments alone with Maddox. He was conscious, although he was weak and in pain.

Rose stroked Maddox's face. "You're going to be okay, Maddox. You have to be. I love you and I need you." She pressed his hand to her stomach. "*We* need you."

"Don't worry, darling," Maddox murmured. "I have too much to live for to give up."

A spark of envy ignited inside Roan. Rose was pregnant. The love between the couple was so strong that it made him ache to have a woman feel the same about him.

Megan's face flashed behind his eyes and nearly knocked the breath from his lungs.

Rose kissed Maddox, then turned to him. "Your turn."

Roan put thoughts of Megan on hold as he stepped up beside Maddox's bed. "What happened?"

"I cornered him, and he opened fire," Maddox said. "I fired back and hit him in the shoulder and leg."

"Did he talk?" Roan asked.

Maddox shook his head. "Not yet. They were

going to do surgery. A deputy is guarding him 24/7. I want you to interrogate him."

"You got it," Roan assured him.

"Thanks." Maddox gritted his teeth. One of the machines beeped indicating his blood pressure was dropping, and the nurse rushed to Maddox's side.

"The doctor's ready to get this bullet out." She turned to Roan and Rose. "Time for you to leave."

Rose blinked back tears as she kissed Maddox again. Roan hesitated before he left the room. Maddox deserved to know that his father was murdered. He'd probably be furious that Roan had kept the truth from him.

But it would have to wait until he was stable.

MEGAN SPENT THE next two hours trying to comfort Rose and Mama Mary. Persuading Rose to tell her the story of how she and Maddox had met and fallen in love served as the perfect distraction.

Roan seemed agitated, but he'd also retreated into a silent, brooding state that made her feel helpless. She'd tried talking to him, but he didn't seem to want to talk.

He made a couple of phone calls, then stood at the edge of the waiting room as if he didn't belong with Rose and Mama Mary.

Or maybe this situation just reminded him of sitting by his mother's bedside before she died.

"If Maddox hadn't saved me, I don't know where I'd be right now," Rose said softly.

Megan squeezed her hand. "I'm sure he feels like you saved him. That love will help him pull through now."

"I hope so," Rose said.

"It will," Megan said with conviction.

The doctor appeared at the doorway to the waiting room. "Family of Maddox McCullen?"

Rose and Mama Mary jumped up and hurried to talk to him. For a brief second, she thought Roan was going to join them, but then he walked to the window and looked out. Megan wanted to ask him what was on his mind, but decided not to push him. He was probably just anxious about the case and Maddox's injury.

Relief filled Rose's face, and she and Mama Mary hugged, both crying. Roan strode over to the doctor and the women then, and Megan followed.

"He made it through surgery and is in recovery. The next twenty-four hours should tell," the doctor said. "So far he's holding his own."

"Can I see him?" Rose asked.

The doctor removed his surgical cap. "When we move him to a room. That'll probably be a couple of hours. If you want to go home and get some rest or something to eat, we can call you."

"I'm not going anywhere," Rose said.

Mama Mary put her arm around Rose. "Me, neither."

Megan wondered what it would be like to have someone be so fiercely loving and protective of her.

If Shelly had lived, would they be close now? Would her father react differently toward Megan?

The day her sister was murdered, a hole had opened up in her, and in him, and they'd never been the same again.

"Call me if you need me," Roan told Rose and the older woman. "I'm going to have a talk with Romley."

"Tonight?" Mama Mary asked. "Son, don't you think it's too late? I'm sure Maddox will understand if you wait till morning."

Roan glanced at the clock, 2 a.m. If the man underwent surgery, he was probably in Recovery. "You're right. I'll go first thing in the morning."

Megan said goodbye to both of the women, her chest squeezing as they hugged her and thanked her for being with them.

It had been a long time since anyone had made her feel so welcome and wanted.

THE THOUGHT OF Maddox dying had done something to Roan. Even though Maddox didn't know it, they were blood kin. Roan had developed a healthy dose of respect and admiration for him both on the job and off.

As he parked in front of Megan's house, he scanned the perimeter again, then kept up his guard as they entered. Their earlier near-lovemaking taunted him. After the tension of the past few hours, he wanted a release. Wanted to take Megan to bed and finish what they'd started earlier.

Dammit, he wanted hot and fast, to pound his body into hers until she cried out his name in pleasure.

He wanted to go slow and easy and slide her clothes off and savor every minute.

He wanted to make love to her.

He silently cursed.

He couldn't do any of those things because as hard as he'd tried not to care about her, he was starting to have feelings for her.

Nearly losing Maddox tonight had served as a reminder to keep his distance from Maddox and Megan.

She looked up at him with that sweet seductive gaze as they walked into her den, and he gruffly ordered her to go to bed and get some sleep.

Hurt flickered in her eyes, but he assured himself it was for the best. She didn't argue. She hurried to her bedroom, making him feel like a heel.

Exhaustion tugged at his limbs, and even though he didn't think he could sleep, he stretched out on Megan's sofa. He laid his gun by his side just in case of trouble, then closed his eyes.

An image of Megan lying in bed wearing a flimsy gown—or nothing at all—teased him. He had imprinted that one night in his memory so deeply that he could almost smell the heavenly scent of her body and feel the luxurious strands of her hair as he ran his fingers through the thick mane.

He could practically hear her whisper his name as if she wanted him to come to her.

Furious with himself, he rolled to his side to face the door, a reminder of the reason he couldn't leave. Megan was in danger, and he wouldn't let anything happen to her.

If anyone tried, they'd have to kill him first.

Chapter Twelve

Megan wrestled with the covers, images of Roan tormenting her. She'd thought they'd connected months ago when his mother died, but obviously she'd been wrong. And tonight, she'd thought she'd seen hunger and desire in his eyes.

Was she simply so desperate for a man to find her attractive that she was imagining it?

She hadn't imagined the heat that had ignited between them earlier or the fact that when they'd made love before that it had been explosive. Sensational.

And that it had stirred emotions inside her that she'd never felt before.

Because you're so inexperienced and naive that you misread sex for affection.

She punched her pillow and rolled over and faced the door. Knowing Roan was on the other side was torture.

Irritated with herself, she turned to the opposite side and faced the wall. It didn't seem to make a difference.

She wanted Roan anyway.

ROAN HADN'T THOUGHT he'd go to sleep, but he must have because the phone jarred him awake. At first he was disoriented, and it took him a minute to realize where he was.

And that, in spite of temptation and his ridiculous obsession to be with Megan, he had managed to stay on her couch.

The phone buzzed again, and he retrieved it from the coffee table where he'd also left his gun.

The number for Horseshoe Creek appeared on the screen. His heart leaped to his throat. What if Maddox…no…he couldn't think the worst. Maddox was strong, stubborn…

"Deputy Whitefeather."

"It's Mama Mary."

He held his breath, his pulse thumping. "Maddox?"

"He's okay, I mean he came through the night and the doc said he's going to make it."

Roan exhaled in relief. "That's good news, then." Except she sounded upset.

"Yes, Miss Rose is still there, but I came home to shower and grab a nap. I told her I'd bring by food later, then she could come home and get some rest. Right now, she won't leave his side."

Once again envy stirred inside Roan. Maddox was a lucky man, in more ways than one.

"But something's wrong?"

"Yes," Mama Mary said, her voice quivering. "Someone broke into the house last night."

"What?"

"It's Mr. Joe's office—I mean Mr. Maddox's. Well, anyway, things are all a mess and torn up like whoever did it was looking for something."

"Are you alone?" Roan asked, concerned about the woman. Where was the security Brett had hired?

"No. The foreman is here. When I noticed that the window had been jimmied, I called him and he came right over. But... I'm worried. Why would someone break in?"

"I don't know but I'll be right there." He grabbed his gun and holstered it on. "Don't touch anything in the office. I'll have a crime team dust for prints."

"All right, thank you, Deputy Whitefeather."

He wanted to tell her it was what family did, but he wasn't part of this close-knit group. All he ever would be was Maddox's deputy. Although hopefully Maddox considered him a friend.

That would have to be enough.

He ended the call, then glanced at the door to Megan's room. He had to at least tell her where he was going. Surely she'd be safe here alone until he returned.

Body taut with tension, he knocked softly on her bedroom door. "Megan?"

She didn't answer, so he knocked again, then heard a noise inside. It sounded...as if she was crying.

Terrified someone had broken in through her window, he shoved open the door. She was thrashing at the covers, kicking and clawing at some invisible force.

His lungs tightened and he raced over to her, sank onto the bed and gently grabbed hold of her arms. "Megan, it's okay, I'm here."

She shoved at his hands and released a sob.

He gently shook her. "Megan, wake up, honey, it's just a nightmare. I'm here and you're safe."

She continued to fight, but he cradled her face between his hands and spoke softly again. "Megan, look at me. It's Roan. You're home safe in your bed."

She went very still then, as if his words sank in, but her body was trembling. She released a cry then sank against him, her breathing choppy.

He pulled her in his arms and rocked her back and forth, soothing her with soft words until her breathing grew steady and her cries quieted.

God…he hated the bastard who'd stuffed her in that body bag.

"Megan, are you okay?"

She nodded against his chest, then lifted her head. Her tear-soaked eyes and the remnants of fear darkening the depths tore at him.

"I'm sorry," she said in a raw whisper. "I'm not usually a crier."

He chuckled softly. "Somehow I knew that." He raked her hair from her cheek. "But you're allowed. Someone did attack you last night."

"I know." She shivered again. "I'll be okay, though. I will."

The pride and determination in her voice made him smile again. "I don't doubt that." He stroked her back, once again vowing to find the bastard who'd hurt her. "Listen, I hate to leave, but Mama Mary called."

She instantly straightened, her concern for everyone else taking precedence over her own fears. "Is Maddox okay?"

He nodded. "He's stable. Rose is with him. She won't leave his side."

"It's obvious how much they love each other," she said in an almost wistful tone.

"Yeah. But someone broke into the ranch house."

Megan gasped. "Is everyone okay? Was Mama Mary there?"

"Not at the time, and she's fine. Just shaken. It sounds like they were looking for something in the study. I'm meeting a crime team there."

Megan reached for the covers to get up. "I'll go with you."

He caught her hand. "You don't have to do that. Get some more sleep or take a shower."

"There's no way I can go back to sleep, Roan." She pushed her legs over the side of the bed. "But I can use some coffee and I probably need to get to work."

"Do you really want to go back to the morgue today?"

Her face looked stricken for a moment. "No, but

I refuse to let anyone drive me away from my job. I have to face it sometime."

He admired her courage. "Then let me drive you. We'll pick up coffee on the way to the hospital."

She agreed, and he reluctantly stepped back into the living room while she dressed. If he didn't, he'd forget the case, take her back to bed and chase her nightmares away with the hot pleasure of sex.

But Megan deserved better than that, so he fortified his resolve to keep his hands off her, then phoned Lieutenant Hoberman to request the crime team.

MEGAN WAS SURPRISED to find the chief ME, Dr. Mantle, waiting in her office when she arrived. He didn't look happy.

His round face was red with anger, his eyes bulging behind his bifocals. "Megan, what in the hell is going on?"

Megan folded her arms in a defensive gesture. She'd never seen him so furious. "What are you talking about?"

He motioned for her to shut her office door, and she did, her nerves on edge. What had she done wrong?

"Dr. Cumberland's wife called me upset. She thinks you're trying to ruin her husband's reputation before he retires."

Megan shifted, choosing her words carefully.

"She also called me, Dr. Mantle, but I assure you I'm not out to hurt Dr. Cumberland. I admire his work and know how much he cares about his patients."

"But you questioned the autopsy results and went behind his back and had samples retested."

Megan sucked in a sharp breath. "First of all, I was just doing my job. When I first read the report, I noticed something odd about the tox screen. I mentioned it to Dr. Cumberland and he acted like I'd made a mistake, then he showed me a contradictory report that had been sent to his office."

Dr. Mantle ran a hand over his balding head. "So there was a mix-up in the reports?"

"That's what he said," Megan replied. "But with contradictory tox screens, I had to run another test to make sure."

"And you did?"

"Yes, with another sample I preserved." She paused. "Isn't that what you would have done?"

He removed his glasses, rubbed at his eyes, then put them back on his face and adjusted them.

"Wouldn't you?" Megan pressed.

He coughed, obviously stalling. "Yes, I guess I would. But Dr. Cumberland says you implied that he was incompetent."

"Oh, my God," Megan said. "That's not true. I respect him. I'm not sure exactly what happened with those two reports, but I couldn't be satisfied without verification."

"Why was it so important to you?"

"Because the tox report indicated that Joe McCullen was poisoned."

His eyes widened beneath his glasses. "You're saying he was murdered?"

"That's what the report indicates. And," she said, her voice raw with memories of her attack, "last night someone knocked me unconscious, put me in one of the body drawers and warned me that if I didn't stop asking questions about McCullen's death, that he'd kill me."

Dr. Mantle staggered backward against the desk. "You're serious?"

"I wouldn't joke about this. I've already talked to the deputy sheriff. He's investigating Mr. McCullen's murder. But this is strictly confidential. He hasn't told the McCullen sons yet."

"Oh, Megan. No wonder the Cumberlands are upset." He wheezed a breath. "You're good, I admit that. And I appreciate your initiative. But you are not to disparage Dr. Cumberland in any way. I don't want this office liable, and I certainly don't want you to ruin that nice man's reputation just as he's close to retirement."

Megan bit her tongue to stifle a sharp retort. Wasn't the truth more important than the man's reputation?

"Besides, Dr. Cumberland was Joe McCullen's friend. I'm sure if anyone wants the truth it's him."

Megan nodded, although if that was true, why not thank her instead of sending her boss to ream her out?

MADDOX WONDERED HOW Megan was handling going back into the morgue after her close call the night before. She was strong and tough, but that experience would have shaken anyone.

He pulled down the drive to the ranch house, morning sunlight dotting the green pastures and hills with golden light. The rain the night before left droplets on the leaves and grass that fell as the wind shook the limbs.

Although even with the beauty of their land, the McCullens had trouble.

He parked and jogged up the steps to the porch. Mama Mary met him, wringing her hands together. "Thanks for coming, Deputy Whitefeather. I didn't want to bother the boys with this, not when they're all worried about Maddox."

"I understand. But you will have to tell them." Just like he had to tell them about their father. And soon.

"Is anything missing?" Roan asked.

Mama Mary led him inside. "Not that I can tell, but Maddox will have to look in the office and safe to make sure."

They crossed the entryway into the office. He

scanned the room, noting the papers scattered around, the open desk drawers, the wall of family photos...

"I didn't touch anything," Mama Mary said.

Roan yanked on a pair of latex gloves. "Do you mind if I look around?"

"Of course not. I just don't understand who's doing this. Who set those fires. It has to stop."

"Don't worry," Roan assured her. "I'll get to the bottom of it."

"Thank goodness you're here." She yawned and rubbed her head with her fingers. "I think I may have to lie down a bit."

The poor woman had been up all night. "Get some rest. I'll let the crime team in and we'll lock up when we leave."

She thanked him, then shuffled from the room.

Roan began to comb through the office. The files on the desk included records of cattle sales, horses that had been bought, expense reports and a business plan the brothers must have put together for further expansion.

He searched the desk drawers and found other information related to the ranch's operation. But wedged between the wooden bottom of the drawer and a corner, he felt the edge of something stuck.

Curious, he yanked at it and realized it was a business card. He pulled it free and skimmed the card.

Barry Buchanan, Private Investigator.

He frowned, wondering if the man worked for the McCullen brothers—or if he'd worked for Joe.

He entered the PI's number in his phone. There was one way to find out.

His thoughts took a dark turn. What if Joe had suspected that someone wanted him dead?

Chapter Thirteen

Roan punched the number for the private investigator, Barry Buchanan. The phone trilled three times before a woman answered.

"Hello."

He'd expected a business greeting. Did he have the right number? "This is Deputy Roan Whitefeather from Pistol Whip. I'm calling for Mr. Buchanan. Who am I speaking with?"

"His wife, Carrie."

"I see. Is the number for his private investigating firm?"

"Yes, but his business is closed," the woman said tersely. "I can refer you to another agency."

"No, I don't need a reference. I wanted to speak to him personally. Is there another number where I can reach him?"

A long awkward pause followed. "I'm afraid not. My husband died two weeks ago."

Roan tensed. "I'm sorry to hear that. Do you mind telling me what happened?"

"A car accident, or at least that's what the sheriff said."

Suspicion laced her voice, making him more curious. "I'm sorry, ma'am. You don't believe it was an accident?"

Another pause. "No. The sheriff said Barry's brakes failed, but my husband was a stickler for keeping his car in tip-top shape. His father owned an auto shop and he worked for him for years."

"What do you think happened?"

"I think someone tampered with his brakes."

Roan tensed. "Did Mr. Buchanan have any enemies?"

"My husband was a private investigator, Deputy Whitefeather. Of course he ticked off some deadbeat cheating husbands and wives. And that's only a few of the cases he worked on."

"You think one of the cases he investigated got him killed?"

"That's exactly what I think. Although the sheriff here doesn't agree."

Under the circumstances, Roan had to take her seriously.

"Why are you interested in my husband's business?" she asked.

The CSI van rolled down the driveway, and Roan acknowledged them with a flick of his hand. "I thought your husband might have worked for a murder victim I'm investigating."

"Well, I don't know details about Barry's cases. And he never told me his clients' names."

"Would you mind if I stop by his office and look at his files?"

Her breath hitched. "I guess not. That is, if you'll do me a favor."

"What kind of favor?"

"If you find something suspicious, someone who held a grudge against Barry enough to kill him, you'll let me know."

"I promise I will, ma'am."

She agreed to meet him after lunch, and he hung up and went to greet the CSI team.

WITH NO AUTOPSIES to perform, the morgue was eerily quiet. A fact that only reminded Megan of the night before and that someone had nearly killed her.

She made a phone call to follow up on Tad Hummings's brother and spoke to the prosecutor who'd tried the man's case. His name was Gerard, and she admired and respected his opinion.

"There were witnesses, the evidence was clear. You didn't make a mistake, Megan."

"Has his brother been a problem?" Megan asked.

"His brother is a mean drunk, but he's also a coward. He doesn't have the guts to follow through on anything. He's just a bully who likes to throw his weight around."

He had plenty of that—he must have weighed 275.

"Do you want to file a complaint against him?"

"No," Megan said. "I just…wanted to make sure he wasn't dangerous."

His breath echoed over the line. "You're not telling me something, Megan. What's wrong?"

There was a lot she wasn't telling him, but she didn't feel like spilling her guts now. Especially with no proof. "It's nothing, Gerard. It's just that…well, the day after I ran into him, I was in a crowd and I thought someone pushed me into the street. But I probably just stumbled."

"What the hell, Megan? Why didn't you call me?"

"I told the deputy sheriff in Pistol Whip," she said. "So no need to call in the cavalry."

"Just to be on the safe side, let me check up on the brother. What day did this incident in the street happen?"

Megan gave him the date and time. A second later, Gerard cleared his throat.

"Megan, Hummings didn't push you. He couldn't have."

"Why do you say that?"

"He was arrested on a DUI the night before and spent the next two days in jail before he made bail."

Megan went still. If Hummings hadn't pushed her, then someone else may have. An eerie chill swept over her. Maybe the same person who'd attacked her last night…

MADDOX MET LIEUTENANT HOBERMAN back inside the ranch house's office. "Did you find anything?"

"A few prints, but considering the fact that the sheriff and his brothers probably all use this office, I'll have to run a comparison."

Roan showed him the private investigator's business card. "Mama Mary had no idea what the intruder was looking for, but I found this PI's card. I called the number to see if he was working for Joe, but his wife answered and said he's dead."

"You think they're connected?"

"It's possible. I think it's time to talk to Maddox." His keys jangled in his hand. "I'm going to the hospital to question Romley, then I'll drop in on Maddox."

Hoberman agreed to let him know as soon as he found anything, and then Roan drove to the hospital. A guard stood at the man's hospital room door, so Roan identified himself.

"You can take a break and grab some coffee or a bite to eat if you want."

The guard nodded, then walked down the hall, and Roan let himself inside Romley's room. The man was hooked up to an IV and a heart monitor. Bandages wound around his thigh and shoulder. His face was pale, dirty-blond hair disheveled, eyes closed.

Roan didn't bother to try to be quiet. His boots pounded the floor as he crossed the room. Romley opened one eye, anger glinting. "I'm not in the mood to talk, just in case you're wondering."

"You shot the sheriff," Roan said. "If you want leniency on that charge, you'd better get in the mood."

Romley groaned as he tried to sit up in the bed. "I need a lawyer."

"Yeah, you do," Roan said. "And I need some answers."

"I got rights," Romley said in a low growl. "That means I don't have to talk to you."

"No, you don't," Roan said. "But as I mentioned, if you want leniency you should cooperate." He crossed his arms and glared down at the man. "Did you set those fires at Horseshoe Creek?"

Romley rubbed at his leg. "I talk, you gonna cut me a deal?"

"That depends on what you have to say."

Romley twisted his mouth into a grimace. "I shot the sheriff in self-defense."

Roan laughed. "Nice try, but that's not gonna fly. You had a warrant out for you. You ran, then resisted arrest." He made a clicking sound with his mouth. "You're racking up the charges."

Romley rubbed at the bandage again. "Gates hired me and Hardwick to keep an eye on Horseshoe Creek's operation and report back what the McCullen men were doing."

"So you reported that Brett was building his equine operation. Adding barns and stock."

Romley nodded.

"Then what?"

"Then…hell, he told me to do something about it."

"Gates paid you to set the fires?"

Romley shrugged, then winced as if the movement caused him pain. "He said there'd be a big bonus if I slowed down their progress."

"So it was your idea to set the fires?"

Romley looked away. "I needed the money."

"You needed money bad enough to commit arson? What if someone had been inside those barns or the house? You could have killed one of the McCullens or their housekeeper."

"No one was supposed to be home that night," Romley said.

"But they were," Roan said. "And what about those horses? How inhumane are you?"

"I only set fire to the empty one." Romley's tone grew defensive. "I figured the McCullens would put it out before it spread and no one would be hurt. The financial damage would have set them back, that's all."

"What about Arlis Bennett? Was he working with Gates?"

Romley clammed up. "I don't know. Gates wasn't exactly my buddy, you know. He paid me. I did what he said."

"Did he pay you to kill Morty Burns and his wife?"

Romley cut his gaze back to Roan. "What the hell are you talking about?"

"Arlis's cousin Morty was in a lot of debt. We think he worked for Gates, too. That he and his wife were murdered because they had information that could expose all of you and send her brother Arlis to jail."

"Listen here," Romley said. "I don't know anything about that. Like I said, I was a hired hand."

"You were a hired killer," Roan said. "You shot Morty and Edith Burns. And you killed Joe McCullen for Gates."

Romley nearly came off the bed. "You're crazy. I didn't kill anyone."

"You expect me to believe that? You shot Sheriff McCullen."

"That's different," Romley said. "He was after me. But I didn't kill anyone. And you're not going to railroad me into prison on a murder rap."

Roan studied him, searching for the truth. He would ask the ballistics lab if the gun that shot Maddox was the same type that had killed the Burnses.

But if Romley hadn't killed the Burnses or Joe McCullen, who had?

MEGAN RECEIVED A text from Roan saying he intended to tell Maddox about his father. He wanted her to join him.

She dreaded the conversation, but Maddox deserved to know the truth. He might even be able to help. After all, Maddox had lived with his father, so he'd probably know who else had visited him.

Still nervous about the attack, she kept her eyes peeled for trouble as she hurried to the floor where Maddox was. She found Rose at the coffee machine. She looked exhausted, but she still offered Megan a smile.

"How is he?" Megan asked.

"Sore, but stable," Rose said. "At least he's out of the woods."

"You should go home and rest, Rose."

"I will." She stirred sugar into her decaf coffee. "I just couldn't bear to leave him yet." She shrugged, a blush staining her cheeks. "I'll go home tonight."

"He's lucky to have you," Megan said.

"We're both lucky."

Megan sighed, wishing Roan felt that way about her.

"What are you doing here?" Rose asked as if she suddenly realized that there was no reason for the ME to visit.

"Roan is on his way. He talked to Romley about the shooting. And there's more information he had to discuss with Maddox."

"I hope they finally figure out who's trying to hurt the family," Rose said. "Maddox and his brothers lost a lot. First their mother, then their father, then there was the trouble with Barbara and Bobby. And now the sabotage with the ranch."

Guilt tugged at Megan. There was still the bomb Roan had to drop about his father's murder.

Roan appeared then, his big body filling the space.

"You have news?" Rose said.

"I just talked to Romley. He admitted that he set the fires. Gates was behind it."

"What about the Burnses?" Megan asked.

Roan shook his head no.

"Who are they?" Rose asked.

"If you come in with Maddox, I'll fill you in."

"Dr. Cumberland is with Maddox now," Rose said.

Megan's pulse jumped. Roan frowned, then turned and strode down the hall. She and Rose followed.

As soon as Roan opened the door, Maddox's angry voice boomed into the hall.

"What do you think you're doing, Whitefeather?" Maddox shouted. "You find out my father was murdered, and you don't tell me?"

Chapter Fourteen

Roan silently cursed.

His gaze met Dr. Cumberland's. Dammit, the doctor had already broken the news to Maddox.

"I'm sorry, Deputy Whitefeather, but I felt it was my duty to tell Maddox what I knew about his father. He had a right to know."

Anger shot through Roan, but he tamped down a reaction. After all, the doctor was a friend of the McCullens. Maybe he had felt compelled to inform Maddox.

"Why the hell didn't *you* tell me?" Maddox asked, his voice gruff.

"I was coming here today to do just that," Roan said, although judging from Maddox's look of disbelief he realized that argument sounded weak. "But I wanted to verify my information before we talked. And then you were shot and I couldn't tell you last night."

Maddox planted his fists on his sides, pressing them into the bed to sit up. "So it's true?"

Roan gave a clipped nod, then glanced at Megan.

She offered him a sympathetic look, then spoke. "Actually, I brought my suspicions to the deputy."

"You did?" Maddox said in a gruff tone.

"Yes. I detected something suspicious in your father's autopsy, but—" She glanced at the doctor, and Roan wondered if she'd confess that Dr. Cumberland had implied that she'd made a mistake.

"But what?" Maddox asked.

"But there were two contradictory reports, so I ran a third test to verify the information. You were out of town so I contacted your deputy and relayed my findings."

Rose moved over to stand by Maddox and laid her hand on his shoulder in a comforting gesture.

Maddox inhaled sharply. "What exactly were those findings?"

Roan forced a neutral tone to his voice. Maddox couldn't know how personal this case was to him. "Dr. Lail found poison, specifically cyanide, in your father's tox screen."

Maddox stared at him, stunned. "Cyanide?"

"That's correct," Megan said.

"I'm so sorry," Dr. Cumberland said, his voice cracking. "Your father was so sick that I didn't notice the signs. That is, if there were any." He wiped a handkerchief over his sweating head. "When your father complained of nausea, I assumed it was his illness coupled with a reaction to the pain medication."

Which made sense, Roan had to admit.

"I feel terrible." Tears leaked from the doctor's eyes. "Maybe if I'd known, I could have bought him a little more time."

"Don't blame yourself," Maddox said to the doctor. "But I don't understand. Why would someone kill my father when he was already dying?"

"That's the reason I wanted to investigate before I came to you," Roan said.

"Do my brothers know about this?" Maddox asked.

"No, of course not. I was going to talk to you as soon as I had something concrete."

"And do you?" Maddox asked.

Roan sighed. "Not exactly."

"What does that mean?"

Roan jammed his hands in his pockets and glanced at the doctor. "Maybe we should discuss this in private."

Maddox studied him for a moment then agreed and asked Cumberland and Rose to step outside.

Roan waited until they'd left before he spoke again.

"I questioned Barbara about the poison, but she seemed shocked when I implied that someone hurt Joe. I haven't spoken with Bobby, although of course Barbara defended him."

"You suspected them because?"

"I thought your father might have planned to change his will to cut them out. If they found that out, it would have been motive."

"True."

"But your father's lawyer claims Joe had no intention of changing his will. He insisted that Barbara and Bobby be taken care of."

He drew a breath. "Arlis Bennett and Gates are top on the list, but so far I have no proof that they poisoned your father. Stan Romley confessed that he set the fires at Horseshoe Creek. He said Gates paid him to keep tabs on the farm and instructed him to do whatever was necessary to slow down your progress."

"Son of a bitch," Maddox muttered.

"There's more," Roan said.

Maddox released a tired sigh and dropped his head back against the stack of pillows. "What else?"

"Gates pointed the finger at another man named Clark. He said that your father refused to give Clark water rights and that eventually caused him financial trouble. That your father forced him to sell."

"So he had reason to hate my father. Or at least in his mind he did."

"It appears that way. I'm going to investigate him, too."

Maddox pinched the bridge of his nose.

"There are a couple of other developments," Roan continued. "Arlis Bennett's sister Edith and her husband were murdered. I'm not sure their deaths are related to your father's death or the fires, but both were shot with a .45, so it's definitely a possibility that they're connected."

"Edith?" Maddox asked.

Roan nodded.

"She used to visit my father a lot," Maddox said. "She and my mother were friends way back in the day."

Mama Mary had said something similar. If Edith had been friends with Maddox's mother, surely she wouldn't have hurt Joe. Would she?

"I talked to Mama Mary about your father's regular visitors," Roan said. "Of course Dr. Cumberland, Bobby and Barbara. Edith came, too. And your foreman."

"He would never hurt Dad," Maddox said. "He's the most loyal man I've ever known."

"But Barbara and Bobby might have," Roan said. "I found fertilizer at Barbara's. It contains cyanide."

"But if the same person killed my father and the Burnses," Maddox said, "it couldn't be Barbara or Bobby. They're both locked up."

"True. There's something else," Roan said, knowing he had to make full disclosure.

"Go on."

"Someone knows we're looking in to your father's murder and that Megan had a part in it. She was attacked and almost murdered last night."

The protective instincts of the McCullens darkened Maddox's face as he looked at Megan. "Are you all right, Dr. Lail?"

"Yes, but call me Megan. Please."

Maddox studied her for a second then nodded.

Roan folded his arms. "This morning Mama Mary called. Someone broke into your house, into your father's office."

Maddox made a move to get out of bed, but Roan shook his head. "She's all right, Maddox. I talked to her. She's safe."

"Then why did they break in? More sabotage?"

"I don't think so," Roan said. "I think they were looking for something."

"Looking for what?"

"I was hoping you might know. Were there any deeds in question? Any bank accounts or transactions that looked suspicious? Did your father keep cash in his safe?"

"No, none of that."

Roan removed the private investigator's business card from his pocket and offered it to Maddox. "I had a crime team dust for prints. In the desk, I found this card. Do you know who this PI is?"

"No. I didn't hire him." Maddox frowned as he skimmed the card. "And I don't recognize his name."

"Do you know why your father might have hired him?"

Maddox wrestled with the sheet as if to get out of bed again, but Roan firmly held his arm. "I know you're upset, but you have to rest, Maddox. I can handle this."

"My father was murdered and this man might know the reason. I have to talk to him."

Roan cleared his throat. "I'm sorry, but that's not going to happen."

"Why the hell not?"

"Because he's dead," Roan replied.

A tense silence fell.

"How?" Maddox asked, frustration in his voice.

"Brakes failed on his car. His wife said it was ruled an accident, but—"

"She thinks he was murdered?" Maddox filled in.

Roan nodded. "When I leave here, I'm meeting her at her husband's office. She agreed to let me look through his files."

Maddox rubbed his eyes again. "Dammit, I want to help."

Sympathy for his half brother settled in Roan's chest. "I understand. But I swear that I'll find the truth, Maddox. I owe you for giving me a chance to prove myself in this town." He owed his father, too, although Joe McCullen had never done a thing for him.

Still, he was his biological father and Roan didn't intend to let his killer go free.

MEGAN FELT FOR MADDOX. But the questions kept adding up. There were too many to dismiss anything as coincidental. Too many that seemed to be connected for them not to be.

She was a woman of science. Concrete evidence. Proof.

Rose came back in, and Maddox quickly filled her in.

"Trust me, Sheriff," Roan implored Maddox. "I'll find the answers for you."

"Let him handle the investigation," Rose said softly. "You have to rest, honey."

Maddox winced at her endearment, but his hand was shaky as if his injury was wearing on him. He had lost a lot of blood.

"Only if you keep me abreast of what you find every step of the way," Maddox said. "I may have been shot, but I'm not dead. And this is *my* father we're talking about."

Megan bit her lip at the spark of anger in Roan's eyes. She didn't quite understand it, except that sometimes prejudice still existed, and maybe he'd had to struggle to get where he was.

"I'll call my brothers," Maddox said. "Ray is a PI. Maybe he's heard of this guy."

"Let me know what he says." Roan's phone buzzed, and he checked the number, then answered. "Deputy Whitefeather." A pause. "Yes. All right, thanks."

When he hung up, he sighed. "Romley's gun, the bullet that he shot you with—it's not the same as the one that killed Morty and Edith Burns."

"So someone else killed them," Maddox said as if thinking out loud. "Maybe Arlis?"

"You think he'd kill his own sister?" Megan asked.

Roan and Maddox exchanged questioning looks. "Hard to say. I don't know Arlis that well."

"Could be Edith discovered that your father was murdered, and she was killed because of it."

ROAN HATED THE seed of resentment sprouting in his gut. He couldn't resent Maddox for what he'd said about *his* father when Maddox didn't know the truth. Still…sometimes he had wondered what his life would have been like if Joe had known about him.

If he'd acknowledged him as his son.

But if Maddox found out now…he'd probably not only fire Roan, but by withholding the truth, Maddox would consider him a liar and be suspicious of his motives.

"I can drop you at home or at a friend's," Roan offered. "With that maniac who attacked you still out there, I don't want to leave you alone."

Megan offered him a brave smile. "I'll go with you. Maybe I can help."

He studied her for a moment, but agreed without an argument, and they hurried to his SUV.

"Are you okay?" Megan asked as he drove from the hospital parking lot.

"Why wouldn't I be?" he said, his voice tight.

Megan frowned. "You seemed upset when you were talking to Maddox. Has there been tension between you two before?"

He shook his head. The last thing he wanted was

for Megan to figure out the truth. To see that he cared, for God's sake.

Anyone he cared about ended up dead.

"Don't read so much into things, Megan. I'm just working a case and trying to keep you alive."

Megan lapsed into silence, and he studied the road, unwilling to pretend that he wanted to talk when the last thing he wanted was for someone to get inside his head.

Twenty minutes later, the tension was still thick as he parked at a small office building in a business park. Several other businesses occupied offices in the complex, and the lot was filled with cars.

He opened the car door, then adjusted his Stetson as he and Megan walked up the sidewalk to the PI's office. When he knocked, a woman with white-blond hair greeted him and introduced herself as Carrie Buchanan.

Roan made the introductions, and he and Megan both expressed regrets for the loss of her husband.

"You believe he died because of a case he was working on?" Roan said.

The fortyish woman toyed with her gold wedding ring. "Yes. Like I told you, Barry was meticulous about keeping his car in good shape."

"Did he mention any specific problem or person?" Roan asked.

"No, but he was agitated lately. He kept getting odd phone calls that upset him, but when I asked about it, he refused to discuss it."

Maybe Roan could look at those phone records, find out more about the calls.

Megan ran her hands through her hair, pushing the wind-tousled strands back behind her ears. For some reason, she'd forgotten the bun today.

It was damn near distracting, too.

That bun had kept him from touching her the first few times he'd seen her. He needed her to wear it again.

"Did your husband ever mention a man named Joe McCullen?" Maddox asked.

"No, like I said, he never revealed his clients' names." She led them inside the office. The front held a receptionist's area divided by a door that must lead to the back and Buchanan's private office.

Roan watched as Megan studied the pictures on the walls. Photographs of the man's credentials, then pictures of several families, smiling and hugging, all nostalgic scenes.

"Mrs. Buchanan," Megan said softly. "Did your husband specialize in any particular type of investigations?"

Mrs. Buchanan adjusted a stack of folders, which didn't need adjusting. They were already neatly stacked. "Yes. He worked with people trying to reconnect with lost family members. Missing kids. Adoptions. Runaways."

Roan scraped a hand over his beard stubble, wondering how that fit with Joe McCullen. He had knowledge of Bobby, his illegitimate son, so he hadn't been searching for him.

But…what if he suspected he had another son? That Joe was looking for *him*?

No…that was impossible. His mother had kept her secret to the end.

"Do you mind if I examine his files?" he asked. "I need to know the reason Joe McCullen hired him."

She gestured toward the door that led to the back, and he and Megan followed her through the hall to an office with metal furniture and hard vinyl chairs. Mrs. Buchanan flipped on the light, then gasped.

Someone had been inside the office and tossed it. Files were strewn all over the office, the file cabinet drawers opened, the files dumped helter-skelter across the floor and desk.

Roan cursed, frustration knotting his belly. He had a bad feeling the file he was looking for was missing.

"My God, it wasn't like this last week," she said in a pained whisper.

Last week he and Megan hadn't been asking questions about Joe McCullen's death.

Chapter Fifteen

Roan scanned the mess of papers strewn across the office with skeptical eyes. An intruder had ransacked the place, obviously looking for something.

Mrs. Buchanan spun the ring around her finger in a nervous gesture. "Who would do such a thing?"

"Someone who didn't want us to see what was in one of your husband's files." Roan surveyed the room and desk. "Your husband had a computer?"

"A laptop."

"Where is it?"

Her gaze swept the room. "I don't know. I thought it was in here."

The laptop was gone.

Megan encouraged the woman to sit down, and Mrs. Buchanan sank into a chair in the corner.

"So he really was murdered?" she said in a haunted whisper.

"I can't say for certain," Roan said.

"Was there an autopsy?" Megan asked.

The woman lifted a shaky hand to push at her

hair. "Yes. He was killed on impact when his car struck a boulder."

"Would you mind if I reviewed that autopsy report?" Megan asked.

Mrs. Buchanan inhaled sharply. "No, that would be fine. I want the truth about my husband's death."

Megan rushed to get the woman a glass of water while Roan yanked on gloves and began to comb through the papers, searching for anything that might have Joe's name on it. Of course, if the killer had stolen the file, he wouldn't find anything.

The PI had organized the files by case number, so he sorted the miscellaneous pages by matching numbers. His wife had been right, most of the cases involved reconnecting birth parents and biological children. Three cases revolved around a kidnapping—all led back to a parent kidnapping a child from the other parent.

So why had Joe been using the PI?

Determined to unearth the answer to that question, he checked the filing cabinet. Most of the files had been dumped on the desk and floor, but a few remained inside, although their contents had been rifled through.

He examined them, but didn't find Joe's. Dammit.

He checked the drawer labeled *M-P*. Empty.

Frustrated, he searched the desk drawers. Sticky notes, pens, stapler, paper clips.

He fumbled through the mess, then noticed a

sticky note with the word "Grace" written on it—a question mark was behind the name.

Grace…

"Do you know anyone named Grace?"

The man's wife shook her head no. "What is her last name?"

"It doesn't say."

"Grace," Megan said in a low voice. "Wasn't that Maddox's mother's name?"

Roan's gaze jerked to Megan's. She was right.

He stared at the slip of paper again, his heart pounding. Joe McCullen's wife had died years ago when the boys were small. Hadn't she died in a car accident?

So had the PI…

Questions ticked through his head, but he had no answers. But the fact that the PI had a question mark by Grace's name made him wonder if whatever Buchanan was looking into for Joe had something to do with his wife.

As soon as they stepped outside Buchanan's office, Megan phoned to request a copy of his autopsy.

"I wish I knew what this means," Roan said.

"Maybe Maddox will have some insight."

"I hate to bother him again. He needs rest to recover."

Megan gently rubbed Roan's arm. "Maddox would want to know, Roan. You heard him earlier. This is about his father, and now…maybe his mother. You can't not tell him."

A muscle ticked in his jaw. "You're right."

The sky had darkened with the threat of another storm, and the wind had picked up, swirling leaves and dust across the parking lot. Shadows played across the sky as the clouds rolled and shrouded the remaining sliver of sunlight.

Megan's phone buzzed that she had an email as they climbed in the car. She checked it and found the autopsy report.

She clicked to open the attachment.

The medical examiner who'd performed the autopsy was a doctor named Lindeman. She skimmed the results of the cause of death—head trauma. His brain had swollen with blood from the impact of the collision. Other lacerations, bruises and a broken femur, ribs and collarbone. Glass fragments pierced his skin, one had embedded in his leg causing more blood loss.

So far the injuries were consistent with the accident.

She skimmed further, though, and frowned at the tox report. "It says here that the doctor found a high level of alcohol in his blood."

"Mrs. Buchanan didn't mention that he'd been drinking."

"No, she didn't." Megan massaged her temple with two fingers. "Maybe the ME decided to spare her the detail."

"Could be. But with her suspicions, we have to ask."

"I'll call her."

"And I'll phone the sheriff who covered the accident and see if he investigated."

Megan punched the woman's number. "Mrs. Buchanan, I'm looking at your husband's autopsy. Did the medical examiner mention that your husband had a dangerous amount of alcohol in his system?"

"No. That can't be. Barry hadn't had a drink in twenty years."

Megan sucked in a breath. "So he was an alcoholic?"

"Yes, a recovering one. He attended AA meetings regularly."

"Perhaps he fell off the wagon."

"No," she said vehemently. "Barry *never* touched alcohol. He messed up when he was young because of drinking and caused an accident that seriously injured a friend. He never forgave himself. He made it his mission to visit schools where he spoke to teenagers about the dangers."

ROAN GRIPPED THE phone and explained to the sheriff in Laramie about his talk with Buchanan's wife. "Did you see the autopsy report?"

"Of course I did," the sheriff said. "The fact that the man had alcohol in his system suggested he lost control. That explained his accident."

"What about the brakes failing?"

"According to the mechanic, there was a slow leak in the brake lines."

"Did you consider the possibility that the brake lines had been tampered with?"

"Why would I? The man was drunk or he wouldn't have been going so fast. If he'd been going slower, he might have been able to stop in spite of the leak."

"The wife seems to think that this wasn't an accident."

"She was in denial," the sheriff said. "Didn't want to believe that her husband was drunk and caused his own accident. She even claimed he didn't drink, but he was an alcoholic. Husbands don't tell their wives everything, you know."

True. But Roan wasn't satisfied.

But the sheriff cut him off and hung up. Roan filled Megan in as he drove from the parking lot. "The sheriff knew about the alcohol, but didn't find it suspicious."

"I know people fall off the wagon all the time, but Barry's wife insisted that her husband never drank. He felt guilty over an accident he caused when he was younger, so he spoke to teen groups about the dangers of drinking and driving."

Roan arched a brow. "If he didn't willingly take a drink, someone could have forced it in him."

"It's possible," Megan said.

Roan mentally contemplated the random pieces

they'd learned so far. Gates and his plan to sabotage the McCullens, Morty and Edith Burns's murders and now Barry Buchanan's murder.

Joe had hired the PI. His wife's name had been scribbled on a sticky note suggesting she had something to do with why Joe had hired him.

The clouds opened up, once again dumping rain on the dry land and slowing him down. Just as he reached the turnoff for the hospital, though, a dark van raced up on his tail. Tires screeched. The car sped up and started to pass him.

Roan scowled and gripped the steering wheel, ready to flip on the siren and chase the bastard. But suddenly the van raced up beside him, and a gunshot blasted the air.

Megan screamed, and he swerved sideways. The bullet missed the glass window by a fraction of an inch.

Another shot rang out, and Roan swerved again. "Get down and hang on, Megan."

She ducked, and he jerked the car to the left to slam into the van. The van swung sideways, tires squealing as it careened forward.

Roan pressed the accelerator, determined not to let him escape, but the van disappeared around a curve.

Roan sped up, but another car pulled out just as he soared over the hill, and he had to brake and swerve to the shoulder of the road to avoid hitting it.

MEGAN TRIED TO compose herself as Roan pulled over and climbed from the car to examine it. He retrieved something from the trunk.

Five minutes later, he climbed back in the front seat and dropped a baggie on the console. "I managed to dig one of the bullets out of the side. I'll have the lab analyze it and see if it came from the same gun that killed the Burnses."

He covered her hand with his. "Are you all right?"

She nodded. "You know, I thought Barbara and Bobby had the most to gain if Joe McCullen was dead, but they can't be doing this."

"You're right. I'm beginning to think Joe's murder didn't have anything to do with them. That whatever this PI was working on for him got them both killed."

Megan considered his suggestion as the storm raged around them and they parked in the Pistol Whip Hospital parking lot.

The rain had slackened, but still water dripped from the trees. She pulled her jacket hood up to shield her from the rain, and Roan settled his Stetson on his head. Then they hurried inside.

Rose and Mama Mary were huddled together in the room with Maddox.

"I tried to get Rose to go home," Mama Mary said as she greeted them, "but she refused to leave."

Maddox laid a hand on his wife's belly. "She's going home tonight if I have to get up and drive her."

Rose laughed softly. "Now I know you're going to be okay. You're getting bossy."

Her casual joke seemed to ease the tension.

Maddox laid his spoon on the tray. "Thanks for the soup, Mama Mary."

She flattened her palms on her big hips. "Well, I couldn't have my boy eating that nasty hospital stuff they call food. If a man wants to get well he needs nourishment."

Maddox chuckled and tolerated her fawning over him. But as soon as she took the tray, he sobered and looked up at Roan. "What did you find out?"

"Actually, I have more questions." Roan explained about his visit to the PI's office and his conversation with the man's wife.

Megan slid into a seat beside Rose and Mama Mary.

"When I spoke to the sheriff who investigated Buchanan's death," Roan continued, "he didn't seem suspicious. But Mrs. Buchanan was adamant that her husband didn't drink. And that he was meticulous about keeping his car in tip-top shape."

Maddox pulled at his chin. "You still don't know why my father hired him?"

Roan glanced at Megan, and she understood his hesitation. Joe McCullen had one illegitimate son with another woman. Could he possibly have had another?

"AT THIS POINT, we don't know, but Buchanan specializes in connecting families with lost members."

"You mean like adoptions?"

"Yes. He's handled a couple of kidnapping cases, but mostly works with adopted children or birth parents trying to find one another."

Maddox wheezed a labored breath. "But that makes no sense. Dad knew about Bobby."

The air grew hot with tension. Finally Maddox looked at Mama Mary. "You knew about Bobby. Did Dad have any other indiscretions?"

Roan fisted his hands by his sides. That was how Maddox would look at him—as an indiscretion. A mistake.

"No, Joe didn't have another affair, if that's what you're asking. I told you, your folks were going through a rough patch when that happened." She puffed up her chest. "Your daddy loved Ms. Grace. But she was extremely depressed over losing the twins."

"I knew about them," Maddox said, "but not that Mama was that depressed."

"Speaking of your mother," Roan said, his pulse hammering at the defensive look in Maddox's eyes. "I found a sticky note with her name on it in Buchanan's desk drawer."

"My mother's name," Maddox said beneath his breath. "I don't understand."

"Someone broke in and ransacked Buchanan's office. If he had a file on your father, it was gone."

"So we're back to nothing," Maddox said, his voice gravelly with frustration.

A dozen questions settled in the air. Mama Mary made a low sound in her throat.

"You said Mr. Joe hired this man. And that he had Ms. Grace's name on a sticky note."

Roan swung his head her way. "That's right."

Mama Mary wrung her hands together. "Oh, my word...it can't be."

Roan's chest thumped. Maddox pushed himself straighter in the bed, although the movement cost him and he clutched at his bandaged torso.

"What is it, Mama Mary?" Maddox asked.

The sweet woman's eyes looked troubled. "I... don't know. I can't be sure..."

Rose patted her hand. "It's okay, Mama Mary. Did you remember something?"

The older woman nodded, worrying her bottom lip with her teeth. "It's just that Ms. Grace, she was so upset about losing the babies. They were both boys you know."

Pain wrenched Maddox's face. "Go on."

"Like I said, she was depressed and she wasn't sleeping at night. She kept saying her babies couldn't be dead, that she heard them crying for her."

A chill went through the room. Judging from the strained expression on everyone's face, they felt it, too.

"I thought she was just in denial." Mama Mary dabbed at her eyes as she looked at Maddox. "She loved you boys so much. You all and your daddy were her life. And she wanted those two other little babies so bad."

"What happened, Mama Mary?" Maddox asked in a gruff voice.

"Dr. Cumberland said Grace was suffering from depression. Postpartum and grief, it was eating her up, so he gave her some medication."

"She was drinking on top of that?" Maddox asked.

"That's what he said the night she died." She wiped at the perspiration trickling down the side of her face. "But the night before… I heard your mama and daddy arguing."

"What were they arguing about?" Roan asked.

Mama Mary sniffled. "Ms. Grace said she didn't think her babies were dead. That she remembered holding them when they were born and hearing them cry. Then suddenly they were gone. Doc said they died at birth, and Ms. Grace was so traumatized she just dreamed she heard them crying. When he told her they didn't make it, she was so hysterical he had to sedate her."

Anguish flared in Maddox's eyes. Confusion also blended with the shock. "My mother thought her babies were alive?"

Mama Mary nodded, her lip quivering. "That's what they argued about. Your daddy was so worried about her that he called the doc that night. He thought she might be going over the edge."

"But she died the next day in that accident," Maddox said.

Mama Mary nodded. "Mr. Joe never forgave himself."

"So your parents argued about whether the twins survived," Roan said, piecing together the facts. "And before Joe died, he hired Buchanan, a man whose specialty was finding missing children and connecting adopted children with their birth parents."

Mama Mary whimpered. "Do you think he discovered something about those babies? That maybe Ms. Grace was right? That someone stole them from her arms and made her think they were dead?"

Chapter Sixteen

Roan considered the possibilities. If someone had stolen Grace McCullen's babies, and Grace kept probing, insisting they were alive, the kidnapper might have panicked and tried to silence her.

And she *had* ended up dead. With her, the questions had died, as well.

Until recently when Joe had hired Buchanan.

Now Joe and the PI were both dead, too.

Mama Mary sniffed and wiped at more tears. "I can't believe this…all these years, I thought those babies were dead, too. Thought Ms. Grace just couldn't accept that she lost them…"

"We're just speculating right now." Maddox turned to Roan. "But if there's a possibility that the infants were kidnapped, that means I… Brett and Ray and I have two brothers we never knew about."

Roan's throat thickened with the need to confess that he was their half brother, but now wasn't the time. Maybe there never would be a time.

He would have to live with that.

He wasn't doing this to gain favor with the Mc-

Cullen brothers. He was a lawman who believed in justice.

"Poor Ms. Grace," Mama Mary said. "No wonder she was so depressed. If she had reason to think her babies were kidnapped and no one believed her, she must have felt so alone."

Pain lined Maddox's face. "Did she say anything specific about why she thought they were alive?"

Mama Mary rubbed her forehead in thought. "Just that she heard them cry when they were born, then she passed out and when she came to, Doc told her they hadn't made it."

Maddox rubbed at his chest. "I remember Mama being sad for a while, and Dad said she lost the babies, but I was so young I didn't really understand. I do remember them talking about a nursery."

"She had just started it when she lost them," Mama Mary said. "Your daddy painted over it in a hurry, thinking it would help. But it only made Ms. Grace mad."

Maddox seemed to absorb that information. "Because she thought the babies were alive."

Mama Mary nodded. "Losing those boys tore him up, too," Mama Mary continued as though reliving those days. "Then he and Ms. Grace started fighting, and she slipped away."

"That's when he met Barbara," Maddox said.

Mama Mary nodded gravely. "I think he just needed some comfort, but it didn't last long. He loved your mama more than words, and wanted to help her get better."

"Except she couldn't because she believed her babies had been kidnapped." Roan chewed the inside of his cheek. "Where are the babies buried?"

Mama Mary's eyes widened. "Well…they…they didn't bury them. Dr. Cumberland had the babies cremated. He said it would be easier on the family that way."

"What?" Anger hardened Maddox's tone. "Did my parents ask him to do that?"

Mama Mary fumbled with the tissue in her hands. "I don't really know. Mr. Joe and the doc talked behind closed doors. I…assumed that was what your daddy wanted."

"I have to talk to Cumberland." Maddox reached for the phone. "He has some explaining to do."

HE CERTAINLY DID, Megan thought.

And without bodies, she couldn't perform an autopsy to determine cause of death or use DNA to verify that the McCullen infants had actually died.

"Good Lord," Mama Mary muttered. "Here, all this time I thought Ms. Grace took those pills and had a drink and drove into that wall to kill herself."

Maddox scrubbed a hand over his face as he punched the doctor's number.

"So if those twins lived," Megan cut in, "who took them?" She paused, mind spinning with more questions. "And if Grace suspected foul play and was asking too many questions, maybe her death wasn't an accident or suicide."

Hushed murmurs of worry echoed through the hospital room.

Megan waited until Maddox left a message for Dr. Cumberland to call him, that he had questions about his mother and the babies she'd lost. He put the phone down, his face strained.

"Was an autopsy performed on Grace?" Megan asked.

"I don't believe so," Mama Mary said. "Mr. Joe and the doc talked and said they didn't want it coming out that she was drinking and taking pills. That Ms. Grace had suffered enough. He wanted her to rest in peace." Mama Mary gave Maddox a sympathetic look. "Mr. Joe was worried about you boys, too. Pistol Whip's a small town, and he didn't want people gossiping."

"That sounds like Dad." Maddox squeezed Rose's hand, and she rubbed his shoulders.

"So we're looking at the possibility that someone kidnapped the twins, then drugged your mother, causing the accident that killed her," Roan said, summarizing what they were all thinking.

"But who would take those babies?" Rose asked.

A thick silence fell while everyone contemplated that question.

"Someone who either wanted them for themselves," Megan suggested.

"Or someone who wanted to hurt Grace, and possibly Joe," Roan finished. "What about the doctor?"

Mama Mary frowned. "He loved this family. He was distraught over losing the babies, too."

"But if they're still alive, he must know something," Roan pointed out.

"I think he had a young doctor working with him at the time," Mama Mary said. "Maybe he had something to do with it and Dr. Cumberland didn't know."

"I'll find out." Maddox rubbed at the bandage on his chest again. "What if Barbara knew my father before my mother lost the twins? Maybe she thought if she could drive my parents apart by kidnapping the babies, she'd have a chance with Dad?"

Maddox angled his head toward Mama Mary. "Did they know each other before?"

Mama Mary ripped the tissue in her hands into shreds. "Ms. Grace met Barbara at the garden club. Later, I remember hearing your father tell Barbara to stay away from your mother, that it was over between them, that Grace had already been hurt enough."

Compassion for the family engulfed Megan.

Barbara was a gardener. She had access to cyanide—Roan had found it at her house.

Had Barbara pretended to be Grace's friend, then killed her in an attempt to keep Joe for herself?

ROAN SHIFTED, FOLDING his arms. "Barbara is the most viable suspect, but there are a couple of problems. She had the opportunity and means to kill your parents. But someone attacked Megan and threatened to kill her if she didn't leave your father's murder alone. Barbara and Bobby are both locked up, so it's impossible that they threatened her."

"They could have hired someone." Maddox reached for his IV to remove it. "I need to get up and do something."

"You are not going anywhere." Rose put a hand on Maddox's to stop him, and Mama Mary moved to her side for reinforcement.

"Listen to your wife." Mama Mary gestured toward Rose's baby bump. "You need to take care of yourself. You got folks who need you now."

Maddox grunted in frustration, but sank back against the bed. "I hate this. I should be working leads."

"Roan will take care of things," Rose said. "Won't you?"

"Of course." Roan had more reason to find the truth than anyone thought, but he kept that to himself.

"I'll have the IT team dig through Barbara and Bobby's financials to see if they made any large payments to anyone," Roan said. "And I want to talk to Dr. Cumberland."

"He was upset when he left," Maddox said. "He still can't understand how someone poisoned my dad while he was under his care."

Roan gritted his teeth, but said nothing. He had no personal attachment to the physician like Maddox and his family did, so he was more skeptical.

"What about Clark?" Roan asked. "He was bitter about losing his land."

"But that happened long after my mother died," Maddox said.

Still, if Grace McCullen's death hadn't been murder, Clark could have killed Joe. But it was looking more and more like Grace was murdered first, and then Joe discovered something that made him suspicious, hired the PI and then he and the PI were killed because of it.

"Didn't you say Edith Burns visited your father when he was ill?" Roan asked.

Maddox nodded. "A few times. She said she promised my mother that if anything ever happened to her, she'd always look in on us kids."

Close friends did that, but considering the fact that Edith and her husband had been shot to death, it made Roan wonder if there was a connection. Maybe a cover-up that had gone back years.

A cover-up that was about to be exposed when Joe McCullen hired Buchanan.

FEELING ANXIOUS, MEGAN swept her hair back into its bun and pinned it in place as Roan drove toward the doctor's office. She didn't like the train of thought her mind had taken. "If those babies didn't die and were kidnapped, that means Dr. Cumberland had to know something about it."

A muscle jumped in Roan's cheek. "That's what I was thinking. Maddox has to be thinking it, too."

Dr. Cumberland had a private practice in Pistol Whip in the square. Two cars sat in the parking lot. A gray Lexus and a black SUV.

"You've known the doctor through the ME's office. Do you think he's capable of such deception?"

Uncertainty crept through Megan. "I don't know. From what I've seen, he's truly caring and kind to his patients. He listens to elderly people, is patient with children and everyone in town knows him and has been to his office for one reason or another. He's delivered most of the babies in town and he's never had a lawsuit filed against him." She paused. "In this litigious society, that's a miracle."

"Maybe we're jumping to conclusions," Roan said. "Joe could have hired this PI to look into Clark or Gates."

Megan nodded. "But it still doesn't explain why Grace's name was on that sticky note in the PI's office."

"It's possible that there was another Grace."

Megan nodded again, although he didn't sound convinced and neither was she. They knew for a fact that Joe had been poisoned. Maybe Joe had hired the PI because he'd received some kind of threat or suspected someone was trying to hurt him?

Together, she and Roan walked up to the doctor's office and went inside. The receptionist, a gray-haired woman with a kind smile, greeted them. "What can we do for you?"

Roan identified himself and introduced Megan. "We need to speak to Dr. Cumberland."

"I'll let him know you're here. He's with the new doctor now." She pressed an intercom button and announced their arrival. Dr. Cumberland told her he'd be right with them.

"A new doctor?" Megan asked. "Is Dr. Cumberland expanding his practice?"

The woman's smile faded slightly. "No. Dr. Cumberland decided to retire so he's bringing in a replacement."

Roan studied the pictures on the waiting room walls—photographs of babies Dr. Cumberland delivered along with families and individuals he'd treated.

"I thought he wasn't retiring until next year," Megan commented.

"The doc's wife is pushing him to travel more."

Interesting, Megan thought. The timing could be coincidental, although it also could indicate that he wanted to get out of town to escape scrutiny over Joe McCullen's autopsy report.

Perhaps the reason he'd been so upset with her when she'd run the test a third time was because he didn't want anyone to know that he'd doctored the report to hide the fact that his friend was murdered.

THE PHOTOGRAPHS ON Dr. Cumberland's wall chronicled the story of a well-loved, small-hometown doctor who'd served his community since he was a young man.

Roan had to tread carefully or he might wreck an innocent man's life.

Or…expose the truth and tear the town apart with lies and secrets that dated back decades.

The door leading to the offices in back opened, and the older man appeared wearing a worn shirt and dress pants. He looked tired, the age lines around his eyes carving deep grooves into his skin.

A younger man, probably early thirties, with thick dark hair and dressed in Western attire including a bolo tie, appeared beside him.

Dr. Cumberland raised a brow when he saw them, then introduced the doctor as Seth Griffin.

They shook hands and made introductions, and Roan gestured toward the back office. "Can we talk in private, Dr. Cumberland?"

He adjusted his glasses, his face sagging with fatigue, but nodded, and Dr. Griffin left.

Roan and Megan followed Cumberland to his office. He offered coffee or water, but they both declined. Cumberland poured himself a cup of coffee, though, and claimed a seat behind his desk, but his hand shook as he set the mug down.

"Dr. Cumberland, we need to ask you some more questions," Roan began.

"I don't know what's going on with you two,

but I've apologized to Maddox and explained that I don't know how I missed what was happening with Joe."

Roan cut his gaze toward Megan, then back to the doctor. "There's more," Roan said. "We discovered that Joe McCullen hired a private investigator named Barry Buchanan."

Dr. Cumberland's face paled. "What would Joe need a PI for?"

"We were hoping you could explain," Roan said.

"I have no idea."

"I think you do," Roan said, cutting to the chase. "Joe was murdered. So was the private investigator."

The doctor's breath whooshed out. "Good God."

"Buchanan's office was also ransacked, some of his files stolen. The file on Joe McCullen was gone."

"You think the man was murdered because of what he was working on for Joe?"

"Yes," Roan said.

"It probably had to do with that cattle rustling ring," Dr. Cumberland suggested. "Joe suspected someone in the community was stealing from others and was determined to find out who it was."

"That's possible, but I found a sticky note with the word 'Grace' written on it. I think Joe hired the PI because of her death."

"But Grace died in a car accident years ago," the doctor said.

"You didn't request an autopsy on Grace, did you?" Megan asked.

He swung a startled look at Megan. "No, didn't need to. I smelled the alcohol on her, and knew she'd been taking antidepressants. I didn't want to put Joe through any more suffering."

"But autopsies are standard in that kind of situation," Megan pointed out.

Dr. Cumberland's voice took on an edge. "Maybe in big cities where there's lots of crime, but not here in a small town. Not when everyone knew the family. Joe loved Grace, but she was severely depressed. There was no need to drag her name through the mud."

Roan arched a brow. "Grace was depressed over losing her babies, correct?"

Dr. Cumberland drummed his fingernails on his coffee cup. "Yes. But that was understandable. She had two stillborn infants."

Roan and Megan exchanged a look. "Were they stillborn?" Roan asked.

The glare Roan received indicated he'd hit a nerve.

"Yes," Dr. Cumberland said through gritted teeth.

"Tell us about the night they were born," Megan said. "Were the babies premature?"

"Yes, about four weeks, but that's not uncommon for twins. Joe was out of town, had gone to buy more cattle. I called him when Grace went into labor, but he was hours away. He never got over the fact that he didn't make it back in time."

"She delivered at the hospital?" Megan asked.

The doctor shook his head. "No, there was no time. Edith came over and took the other three boys to her house for the night. I wanted to get Grace to the hospital, but her contractions were one on top of the other. I tried to make her comfortable and help her through it, but when I delivered the babies, they weren't breathing. And one of them, well, he was also deformed." Emotions twisted the doctor's mouth. "I tried to resuscitate them, but failed."

"Did you request an autopsy to determine cause of death?" Megan asked.

"Look, it was thirty years ago. Rules and regulations weren't so tight." He shrugged. "Besides, Grace was so distraught. She didn't want anyone desecrating their little bodies, and I respected her wishes."

"Did she hold the babies?" Megan asked.

He shook his head again. "No, like I said she was distraught. I had to give her a sedative to calm her."

"And you had the babies cremated instead of letting the family bury them?" Roan pressed.

The doctor's mouth tightened. "It was what the McCullens wanted. Grace said she didn't think she could bear to look at those tiny graves."

"What happened to the ashes?" Megan asked.

"Joe and Grace scattered them in the pond on Horseshoe Creek."

So there was no chance of testing the ashes.

Roan folded his arms, his voice hard. "Are you certain that's the way it happened?"

"Of course. It was a terrible time. I loved that family and afterward did everything I could to help Grace and Joe mourn their loss."

"I don't believe you," Roan said. "I have reason to think that Grace suspected her babies hadn't died, that someone kidnapped them."

Dr. Cumberland gasped. "That's ridiculous. For God's sake, I was there."

Roan leaned across the desk, hands planted firmly on top, eyes boring into the doctor's. "Exactly."

The man's eyes narrowed to slits. "Just what the hell are you implying?"

"That for some reason you took those babies and gave them to someone else. Maybe for money. Maybe it was someone you knew. Either way, later Grace questioned it, and she was killed because she refused to stop looking for them."

Chapter Seventeen

Dr. Cumberland stood, his nostrils flaring. "I don't like the implications, Deputy Whitefeather. Does Maddox know that you're here making these kinds of accusations?"

Roan met his gaze with a cold stare. "Yes."

That sucked the bravado out of the man. "This is unreal. I've devoted myself to this town and the McCullens were my personal friends. I'd take my own life before I'd hurt one of them."

"Then how do you explain all the inconsistencies and the deaths," Megan interjected.

"We know for a fact that Joe was murdered. We suspect Grace might have been, as well. The private investigator Joe hired was also killed in a suspicious car accident, an accident similar to Grace's." Roan hesitated. "Also, Morty and Edith Burns were shot to death. You knew them, didn't you?"

"Yes, but…" Dr. Cumberland shook his head in denial. "When did that happen?"

"A couple of days ago," Roan answered. "Did you

say that Edith took care of Maddox and his brothers the night Grace gave birth?"

The doctor nodded, although he suddenly looked ill. "Edith and Grace were good friends."

"Then Grace probably confided her fears to Edith."

More questions ticked in Roan's head. What if Edith was killed because she found out that Dr. Cumberland had kidnapped the McCullen twins? Or what if she actually aided in the kidnapping?

"If you want to know who would kill Joe, look at Barbara," Dr. Cumberland said. "She was bitter toward both Grace and Joe."

"We've already questioned her," Roan said. "She claims she would have never hurt Joe."

"But she might have killed Grace." Dr. Cumberland stood, eyes fixed with anger. "Now, I've answered your questions, it's time for you to leave."

Roan planted his hands on the desk again. "There's one more thing, Doctor. The day Megan ran that third test on Joe McCullen's blood, someone pushed her into the street. And shortly after she got the results, someone attacked her in the morgue and threatened her."

Nerves fluttered in the doctor's eyes.

"Other than the lab tech who ran the sample, you were the only person who knew about that test and the results."

A coldness seeped into the doctor's eyes that

struck Roan as guilt. A second later, the doctor swung his hand toward the door.

"Get out, Deputy. I'm done with your accusations."

Roan refused to be intimidated. "Know this, Dr. Cumberland, if you were involved in either of the McCullens' death or the Burnses', or if you're lying about what happened to the twins, I will find out." He leaned closer, eyes pinning the man to the spot. "And nothing had better happen to Dr. Lail. Do you understand?"

Another tense second passed, and then the doctor gave a clipped nod.

But Roan didn't trust him. As soon as he and Megan left the office, he phoned the lab and asked them to examine the doctor's phone and bank records going back three decades.

If someone had paid Cumberland to fake the twins' death, that would be a place to start.

MEGAN WORRIED HER lip with her teeth. "If Barbara had something to do with Joe's death, maybe we should talk to her again."

"She's not going to confess," Roan said. "She's just as defensive as Dr. Cumberland."

"Then talk to Bobby. If his mother killed Joe and he didn't know about it, he might turn on her."

"Good point. Let's pay him a visit."

She struggled to make sense of the situation as he drove to the prison where Bobby was locked up.

He was being held in a minimum-security facility that provided mental health.

"I still find it hard to believe that Dr. Cumberland would deceive the McCullens like that," she said, thinking out loud. "He seemed to genuinely care for them. And no one has ever filed a complaint against him."

Roan scrubbed a hand through his thick, long hair. "You never know what people will do if they're pushed into it."

"What do you mean?"

"It was a long time ago," Roan said. "We don't know what was going on in the doctor's life back then. Hell, what if he and Barbara had had a thing?"

"That doesn't seem likely," Megan said. "But I guess you're right. I just hate to think that he betrayed that family's trust."

They parked at the prison, then cleared security, and Roan explained to the warden that he needed to visit Bobby. "How is he doing?"

"He has his good days and bad days. The therapist is working with him on anger management issues. He's been sober now for weeks, so that helps."

One of the guards led them to a visitor's room, and a few minutes later another guard escorted Bobby into the room. He wore prison garb and was handcuffed, but lacked the shackles. The gray pallor of his skin indicated he hadn't seen much sunshine, and the glint of anger in his eyes indicated he still harbored bitterness toward the world.

"You can remove the handcuffs," Roan said.

Bobby seemed wary, but muttered a thanks when the guard unlocked the cuffs. For a moment, he rubbed at his wrists as if the cuffs had hurt. Or maybe he just hated confinement.

She remembered being confined in that body bag and understood the suffocating feeling of having your freedom stripped away.

"Hello, Bobby, I'm Deputy Whitefeather, and this is Dr. Megan Lail, the medical examiner in Pistol Whip."

Bobby cut his steel-hard eyes toward Megan, and a spark of male appreciation replaced his resentment. "To what do I owe the pleasure?"

Megan forced a neutral expression, determined not to let him bait her. "We need to talk to you about your father."

"My father is dead," Bobby said matter-of-factly.

"Yes, he is," Roan said. "But we know the truth about how he died now."

Bobby's eyes flickered with emotions that Roan couldn't quite define. "What is that supposed to mean?"

"I performed an autopsy on Joe," Megan said. "He didn't die of natural causes. Someone poisoned him."

Bobby gaped at them in shock. "My father was murdered?"

Megan nodded slowly.

"That's impossible," Bobby said. "He was sick. He had emphysema…"

"Yes, he did," Megan said. "But his illness didn't take his life. I found traces of cyanide in his tox report. Someone slowly poisoned him to death."

"Cyanide?" Bobby's voice grew shrill. "But that's crazy." He spread his hands in front of him and stared at his bruised knuckles.

"You had the most to gain from your father's death," Roan said bluntly.

Bobby's head jerked up, rage darkening his face. "You think I killed my own father?"

Megan swallowed hard at the pain in Bobby's voice. Was he lying or was he really shocked by his father's murder?

ROAN NARROWED HIS EYES, scrutinizing Bobby. "Maybe you already knew what your father put in that will and you weren't happy about it."

"But I didn't know," Bobby stuttered.

"Then you thought he was going to change his will and cut you out completely, and that wasn't fair." Roan lowered his voice. "Hell, man, I get it. You were just as much a son to Joe McCullen as Maddox or Brett or Ray, but he never treated you the same. You got bits of his time and attention when he could fit you in."

Pain wrenched Bobby's face.

"I don't blame you for being angry, for hating the McCullens. Joe should have made you a part of his family. He should have given you the riding lessons and the land and his name—"

"Yes, he should have," Bobby growled.

"You visited him when he was sick?"

Bobby nodded. "He apologized, said he knew he'd let me down, but that I had to shape up. Hell, I bet he never talked to his other sons that way. They didn't have to prove they were worthy of being a McCullen like I did."

How could Roan not understand the man's animosity? "Even when he was dying, he didn't acknowledge you to your half brothers?"

Bobby shook his head. "He was ashamed of me."

Roan's heart pitched. Would he have been ashamed of him if he'd known he was his son?

"So you decided to get back at him, didn't you?" Roan asked. "You slipped some poison in his drink and slowly watched him die."

Bobby shot up from this seat, outrage flashing in his eyes. "That's a lie."

The guard stepped forward, stance aggressive, handcuffs in one hand, his other on the gun at his waist. He motioned for Bobby to take a seat.

"Damn this." Bobby glared at the guard, but sank back in the metal chair. He rolled his hands into fists on the table, then took several deep breaths.

"That's total crap. Yes, I was furious at my father, and I never made any bones about the fact that I resent my half brothers. They've never done anything for me. I'm sure they're pissed that Dad included me in the will." His eyes darkened. "Have you considered the fact that maybe one of them wanted to get back at him for his affair with my mother?"

"That makes no sense," Roan replied. "First of all they had no knowledge of you. And secondly, if they did, they would have tried to convince Joe not to include you in the will. Killing him only meant you got your share sooner."

Bobby's face fell. Apparently he hadn't thought his theory through.

"Listen to me." Bobby lowered his voice. "I was mad at my father, but I didn't kill him. Like a fool, I…kept hoping he'd make things right before he died."

Roan chewed the inside of his cheek. The pain and raw hope in Bobby's voice sounded sincere.

"What about your mother?" Megan asked. "Barbara had just as much reason to be angry at Joe as you did."

Bobby twisted his head toward her. "She loved Joe until the end. She would have never hurt him."

"Really?" Roan said. "She was obsessed with Joe for years. She wanted him, but even after his wife died, he refused to marry her."

Bobby's lips thinned into a straight line.

"In fact, we now believe that Grace McCullen might also have been murdered."

"What?" Bobby stuttered.

"Did you know that Grace McCullen was pregnant with twins a few months before she died? That she lost those babies?"

Bobby looked from Roan to Megan, then shook his head. "I have no idea what you're talking about."

"Then I've got a story to tell you," Roan said. "Joe married Grace and had three sons. Later she got pregnant with twins. Somehow Barbara had met Joe and had a thing for him, but she knew he wouldn't leave his wife. So she hires someone to help her kidnap those babies when they're born. Grace and Joe think the babies died, but Grace can't get over it. That was Barbara's plan—she wanted to drive Grace and Joe apart."

"You're crazy," Bobby muttered.

"It worked for a while. Joe hooked up with your mother, and they had you. But Joe still loved his wife and refused to leave her. A few months later when Barbara realized her plan hadn't worked, she decided the only way to have Joe was to get rid of Grace. She discovered Grace was on antidepressants, so somehow she found a way to get some alcohol into Grace. Mixed with the pills, Grace passes out and is killed in what appears to be a car accident."

Roan paused. "But that doesn't do the trick. Joe still won't marry her. He still keeps you and your mother on the side. Barbara puts up with it for years but her resentment grows. Then eventually Joe gets sick. She finds out about the will and is irate at how he left things and poisons him."

Bobby shook his head in denial, but said nothing.

"She took your father from you before his time was up," Roan said, pressing harder. "Maybe if she hadn't, he would have found a way to introduce you to your half brothers."

Bobby's face blanched. "My mother wouldn't have done that."

"Can you be sure, Bobby? Just look at what she did a few months ago. She pulled a gun on Scarlet Lovett and threatened the McCullens."

Bobby looked down at his hands, his face anguished. His breathing was choppy as he stood. A cold resignation framed his eyes as he met Roan's gaze. "I want to see my mother."

Roan's pulse jumped. He was hoping he'd say that. "I can arrange that." He paused. "But only if you let me listen to your conversation."

A vein throbbed in Bobby's neck. "You want me to try to trap my mother into confessing to murder?"

"I want the truth," Roan said. "I think you do, too."

Bobby squared his shoulders, his body ramrod straight. "Fine, set it up. But I'll prove you wrong."

Roan gave a small nod, although Bobby's voice lacked conviction, as if he didn't think that would happen at all.

As if he thought his mother was guilty.

Chapter Eighteen

Sympathy for Bobby welled in Megan's chest. If his mother had murdered Joe and Grace and kidnapped the twins, she would spend the rest of her life in prison.

Bobby would also lose the only parent he'd ever really known.

But at least if Bobby confronted her, they'd learn the truth.

Although it was early evening, Roan didn't want to put off the interview with Barbara until the next day. If he did, Bobby might change his mind. He might also find a way to contact his mother, which could work against getting that confession.

She and Roan stopped and had dinner at the local diner while he arranged the transport and meeting. Two hours later, they sat in a room with a two-way mirror that allowed them to view the conversation between mother and son.

Bobby looked even more agitated than he had when they left him. Barbara looked…excited, happy about seeing Bobby again.

"Son, I'm so glad to see you." Barbara swiped at tears and folded Bobby in her arms. Roan had instructed the guards to remove the handcuffs so the two could talk openly. If the situation spiraled out of control, the guard would step in.

Roan was prepared to back him up.

"Mother, you look…good," Bobby said.

Barbara blushed and shook her head. "Orange has never been my color. And they won't let me have my makeup. It's a travesty."

Megan almost laughed. The woman was harping on her looks when she was locked up for months. If they made this kidnapping or murder stick, she would be inside for the rest of her life.

"I've missed you so much, Bobby. You look good. Although you're a little thin." Barbara fluttered a hand down her cheek, then sank into the metal chair, but kept one hand clasped in her son's.

"The food sucks," Bobby said.

"Well, one day we'll be out and I'll fix you all your favorites again." Barbara pressed Bobby's hand to her cheek. "I dream about that all the time. Making that pulled pork you like and that coconut cake with the three layers."

Bobby looked torn. "Yeah, that'd be great."

"How did you arrange this get-together?" Barbara asked. "Are you getting an early release?"

Bobby had plastered on a smile, but it faded. "No early release, but I'm working through rehab."

"That's good, son. I want you to do well, to get

out and prove to those McCullens that you deserved to be one of them."

"I don't care about being a McCullen anymore," Bobby said.

"But you're inheriting your own piece of land, Bobby. You'll have your own spread one day just like I always dreamed about for you."

Bobby gritted his teeth. "I know, Mom. I need to ask you something."

Anxiety knotted Megan's shoulders as she watched Bobby. She couldn't imagine confronting one of her parents in this kind of situation.

"What is it, honey? You want to talk about your therapy?"

"No, Mother, I want to talk about my father."

Barbara thumbed a strand of hair from her cheek. "All right."

"The police said Dad was poisoned. Did you kill him?"

Barbara gasped. "How can you ask me that, Bobby? You know how much I loved Joe."

"Yes. But I also know how much you hated his wife. The police say she was murdered, too."

"Yes, I hated that woman," Barbara admitted. "And I wanted her to die so I could have Joe, but I didn't kill her."

"Joe was poisoned with cyanide." Bobby leaned closer to her, his voice a conspiratorial whisper. "You kept cyanide, Mother. You used it in your gardening. And you visited Joe multiple times, and you were always making him cookies."

Rage slashed Barbara's face as she pushed herself to stand. "I can't believe you of all people would accuse me of such a thing." She glanced at the guard, then around the room.

"Did you do it?" Bobby asked. "Did you kidnap those twins, then kill Grace so Joe would be with you?"

Barbara went stone-cold still. She turned slowly and looked at the mirror on the wall, then spoke as if she knew they were watching. "How dare you force my son into trying to trap me to confess. I did not kill that damned woman, and I certainly didn't kill Joe." Her eyes turned menacing. "You will pay for turning my son against me. You'll pay."

She flicked her wrist and motioned to the guard. "Now get me out of here. I'd rather be in my cell than visiting with a son who would stab me in the back."

"THAT DIDN'T GO as I expected," Roan said.

"I know you were hoping for a confession." Megan fastened her seat belt as they drove toward Pistol Whip. "But maybe we have it wrong. Maybe Barbara wasn't the killer."

Roan grunted in frustration. "Could be. Everything leads back to Dr. Cumberland and that night the twins died…or disappeared. He could have covered up Grace's and Joe's murders, too."

"But he spent his whole life helping people in this town," Megan continued.

Roan phoned the doctor, but his voice mail picked up, so he left a message.

He hung up, but couldn't get the doctor off his mind. A second later, his phone buzzed. The lab. "Deputy Whitefeather."

"Roan, it's Lieutenant Hoberman. We researched Barbara Lowman's accounts as well as Dr. Cumberland's. There were a few deposits made in Barbara's account that could have raised red flags, except we cross-checked with Joe McCullen's and they match."

"Joe was supporting her and Bobby?"

"Yes, for years."

No surprise there. Would he have helped Roan's mother if he'd known she'd given birth to his son? Or would he have denied having a Native American child? "How about the doctor?"

"His are a little more interesting. His income has been stable, but we dug deep into when he first started practicing."

"He owed a lot of money?"

"That's not it. The year before the twins died, he made a mistake that cost a patient her baby," Hoberman said. "The couple claimed he took some uppers to keep him awake during a delivery. The delivery went south and the baby died. The couple was going to sue, but something changed their mind and the case was dropped."

Roan's chest constricted. "They were paid off."

"Probably. I'm trying to get the couple's names, but it's difficult to access medical files."

Yes, it was. But the incident suggested a motive for Dr. Cumberland to take the McCullen babies. Maybe he was trying to pay the couple off by giving them another child.

MEGAN'S CHEST ACHED as she listened to Roan explain the CSI's findings. "Oh, my God. A mistake like that would have cost him his license, his entire career."

"But it was swept under the rug," Roan said. "Probably for money, or maybe Dr. Cumberland came up with another solution."

"What do you mean?"

"He could have replaced the child with another baby. Or two."

Megan's heart pounded as she considered his theory. Unfortunately, it made sense. If Dr. Cumberland had caused that infant's death, guilt could have forced him to kidnap the McCullen babies.

But to steal a child—no, two children—from his own friends? And why would he have chosen the McCullens?

Because they already had three children…?

Megan stared into the dark woods they passed as night set in. Farm and ranch land spread for miles and miles, the hint of wild in the rugged ground and boulders interspersed between lush pastures.

Birds sailed above treetops, diving for food, and a bobcat darted through the woods.

Roan pulled down a narrow street just outside of Pistol Whip. It wasn't a street, but a long driveway that led through the woods to a private estate.

"Dr. Cumberland lives down here?"

"Yeah, apparently he's done well for himself."

Dr. Cumberland's house was a rustic two-story with a wraparound porch complete with planters and a porch swing. It looked so homey and inviting that Megan couldn't imagine anything sinister inside—especially a small town doctor with deadly secrets.

Roan parked beneath a giant tree with limbs that resembled arms stretching toward the sky. The door swung open before they could make it to the front porch, and Mrs. Cumberland barreled down the steps toward them.

She folded her arms under her ample bosoms, her eyes flaring with accusations. "Where is my husband?"

Megan came to a halt beside Roan.

"Actually, we came to talk to him," Roan said evenly.

The woman huffed. "Well, he's not home. I talked to him earlier and he was upset, said the two of you are treating him like he's a suspect in Joe McCullen's murder." She shook her finger at them. "You should be ashamed of yourselves. After all my husband's done for this town and those Mc-

Cullens. Those boys can't possibly think he'd hurt their father."

"Mrs. Cumberland," Megan said, "we're just asking questions to figure out what happened."

"Because someone did murder Joe McCullen," Roan finished. "We also know that your husband had a case that went bad a few years ago. A baby died. A couple threatened to sue him."

The color drained from the woman's face. "That happened years ago," she said with a confused look.

"What about the night the McCullen twins died?" Roan asked.

One hand fluttered to her heart. "They were stillborn, for God's sake. That wasn't my husband's fault."

Roan cleared his throat. "Actually, we have reason to believe that your husband faked the babies' deaths and gave the twins to someone else."

"What?" The doctor's wife threw up her hands. "That's ridiculous."

Compassion for the woman filled Megan. But if their suspicions were true, her husband had destroyed lives.

"You're going to be sorry you did this," Mrs. Cumberland said. "I'm going to talk to Sheriff McCullen. Maddox would never put up with you treating us like this."

Roan's jaw tightened. "I'm just doing my job."

"A job you never should have been given," she

said. "Why don't you go back to the reservation with your own people?"

Megan's breath caught. She started to say something, but Roan stopped her with a hard shake of his head.

"If you hear from your husband, tell him he can either come in on his own, or I'll pick him up," Roan said in a dark tone. "Either way, as long as I am the deputy sheriff, he will answer my questions."

"Get off my property!" Mrs. Cumberland shouted.

Emotions welled in Megan's throat. She knew some folks still harbored prejudices, but she hadn't expected it from Mrs. Cumberland.

Then again, the woman was shaken up over the accusations they'd made and was probably lashing out any way she could.

It still didn't make it right, though.

Was she so defensive because her husband was innocent, or because she was trying to cover up for what he'd done?

ROAN'S PHONE DINGED with a text as he drove away from the Cumberlands' house. He handed it to Megan. "Read that."

Megan took his cell phone and skimmed it. "It's from Dr. Cumberland. He wants to meet us at the morgue. He's ready to talk."

Roan's heart hammered. "Good. Maybe we'll finally learn the truth."

He pressed the accelerator, veered onto the road leading through town and flipped on his siren. It might not be an emergency, but Megan's life had already been endangered, and finding whoever had threatened her and shot at them was imperative.

Already too many people had died.

Ten minutes later, he swerved into the parking lot and threw the vehicle into Park. Megan was getting out before he could make it around to open the door for her.

He hurried to walk with her, his gaze scanning the hospital parking lot. Bushes lined the exterior, adding greenery and color, but also provided places for a predator to hide.

Footsteps sounded behind them, and he jerked his head to the left to search for trouble, but a man and child were walking toward the entrance, carrying a bouquet of pink roses and a white teddy bear, along with a "Congratulations, it's a girl!" balloon.

Such a happy occasion in the midst of so much death in the town.

The man and child were oblivious, though, hugging and laughing as they hurried inside to welcome the newest member of their loving family.

A pang of longing tugged at Roan, something he'd never felt before. The need for a family.

For a wife and a child of his own.

He glanced at Megan, and an image of her holding his baby son taunted him.

Megan caught his arm as they followed the man

and child in, and he wondered if she might be thinking the same.

She gestured toward the elevator, a reminder they weren't headed to the nursery where new life was being celebrated, but to the morgue where loved ones met with death, murder and grief.

They rode the elevator in silence, then walked down the hall toward the morgue. The dreary paint on the walls needed a new coat, preferably something with color. The lights seemed dimmer down here, and the smell was suffocating—a blend of strong antiseptics and cleaner meant to disguise the more acrid odors of what happened between the cement walls inside, but failed.

This was Megan's world. She was unlike any woman he'd ever known. Tenderhearted yet strong, determined to find the answers for the families grieving for their lost loved ones.

A diamond in the rough.

She swiped her ID card to get inside, then glanced through the window to the autopsy room, but it was empty. The lab was empty as well, indicating the employees had left for the day.

"He must be in my office."

"Dr. Cumberland has a key to your office?"

She shook her head no. "But if he arrived before Howard left the lab, he would have let him in."

Roan nodded, but he didn't like it. This place was creepy. Set away from the main hospital in the far corner of the basement, Megan and her workers were virtually isolated.

Which meant they could be walking into a trap.

Honed for trouble, he pulled his gun and followed her down the short hallway.

When they reached the door to her office, he caught her arm. The door was closed.

Fear clouded her eyes as she looked up at him, and he gently coaxed her behind him and turned the knob. The door squeaked open. Roan held his gun at the ready as he stepped into the doorway.

Darkness bathed the room, but the faint light from the hall illuminated the inside, enough for him to tell that the chair behind Megan's desk was occupied. All he could make out was a man's head, though. No movement.

"Dr. Cumberland?" Megan said softly as she inched into the doorway.

Silence echoed back.

Roan detected the metallic scent of blood.

Dammit.

Roan held out his hand to stop Megan from entering as he flipped on the light. He knew what he was going to find, but the sight of blood and brain matter splattering the walls still made bile rise to his throat.

"Oh, God." Megan's legs buckled.

He caught her and pulled her up against him to shield her from the grisly sight.

Chapter Nineteen

Megan struggled to breathe through the shock. Dr. Cumberland was…dead. In her office.

"Don't touch anything," Roan said.

Megan dug her nails into his arm. "I know the drill, Roan. What…do you think happened? Do you think…he killed himself?"

"I don't know." He handed her his phone. "Call the crime team and stay in the hall."

She found the number in his contacts, keeping her feet rooted to the floor. He didn't have to tell her twice not to go inside.

She'd seen a lot of dead bodies, but she knew this man, had spoken with him, had conferred with him.

Worse, she and Roan had been asking questions. Had they gotten him killed?

The phone rang three times then a man answered. "Lieutenant Hoberman."

"It's Dr. Lail. Deputy Whitefeather asked me to call. I'm with him now."

"What's going on?"

"We're at the morgue, my office. It's Dr. Cumberland...he's dead."

"Good God." The lieutenant released a loud sigh. "I'll get a team and be right over."

She thought she thanked him, but she couldn't be sure. Her eyes were glued to Roan, who'd pulled on latex gloves and was walking around the front of the desk to examine the doctor.

Megan held her breath, her head spinning from the scent of fresh blood.

"He was shot?" Megan asked.

"Yes." Roan scrutinized the scene. "Shot in the temple, close range, right side."

"He was right-handed," Megan said.

"He's holding a .38. I'll have to follow up and see if he owned the gun." He stooped and examined the man's hands, then looked up at her. "Powder burns on his hands indicate he fired the weapon."

Megan's mind spun. "Why would he text you to meet, then kill himself before you arrived?"

"Good question." Roan retrieved his phone, then snapped pictures of the office and the doctor's body position.

"Do you think someone else was here?"

Roan shrugged. "It's a possibility."

That would explain why he died before they arrived. Someone knew he was going to finally talk and wanted to shut him up.

Megan scanned the office. The files she'd stacked on her desk seemed undisturbed, her favorite coffee mug in the same place she'd left it. Her books were in order on the bookshelf, desk lamp in place.

There were no signs of a struggle.

Roan made a low sound in his throat as he peered at Megan's desk, his brows furrowed. "Damn."

Perspiration beaded on Megan's neck. "What?"

"He left a suicide letter on your computer."

Roan read the note aloud.

"Dear Dr. Lail,

I know you and the deputy have been asking questions and you're close to uncovering the truth. My conscience has bothered me for a long time, and it's time I tell the real story about what happened years ago.

I made a terrible mistake earlier in my career and should have performed a C-section on a woman. Complications arose because of it and the woman lost the baby. She and her husband blamed me. I tried to settle with them out of court, but the woman couldn't have more children. Her husband threatened to ruin my career if I didn't help find them another child.

I panicked. I didn't want my career to end. I loved the people in Pistol Whip, and couldn't live with myself and my mistake. So the night Grace McCullen went into labor, I decided to take her babies and give them to this couple.

I realize it wasn't right, but Joe and Grace had three boys already. They had a family, and

I thought Grace would eventually get pregnant again.

But she never recovered from that night. She started asking questions. She said she wouldn't stop looking until she found her missing boys.

I honestly thought she'd mixed the antidepressants with alcohol and had an accident, though. But once you raised questions, I started having doubts myself.

I made some calls, and I think the man I gave the twins to had Grace killed. I also think he poisoned Joe because one day Joe was on a buying trip and came back and told me he'd seen a young man who looked a lot like Maddox. Joe started probing then, wondering if his wife was right. He hired a PI to find the truth.

The man I gave the twins to was Bart Dunn. He won't give up the truth easily, but it's time the McCullen boys knew the real story.

I can't live with these secrets and lies any longer. I left my wife a letter explaining everything. She had no idea what happened. Please tell her that I love her, and I'm sorry for keeping secrets. Most of all I'm sorry I betrayed my friends. If I could go back and change things, I would.

But some mistakes can't be taken back.

Also, let Maddox and Brett and Ray know that I really loved their father and them. I never meant to hurt anyone."

"My God, he really did it." Megan's pained voice echoed across the room. "His poor wife, she's going to be devastated."

"I'm sorry, Megan," Roan said quietly. "I understand that you considered the doctor a friend."

Megan shrugged. "He did have a good side," she said. "He did a lot for the people here in Pistol Whip."

"But he also betrayed one of his best friends, and he hurt Grace McCullen terribly."

"I know. I can't imagine giving birth and losing my child. No wonder Grace slipped into a deep depression." Megan sighed. "If she suspected foul play, and that the twins were still alive and no one believed her, she must have felt so scared and alone."

THE NEXT TWO hours passed in a blurry haze for Megan.

The crime team took photographs, processed her office, made copious notes on the scene and their findings and searched for forensics. They dusted her computer for prints to verify that Dr. Cumberland had typed the note and that it hadn't been written by another party.

Under the circumstances, she phoned the chief ME to perform the autopsy.

Megan's stomach roiled as they finally moved the doctor's body from her office and carried him to the morgue.

"We have to notify Mrs. Cumberland," Roan said.

"I can take care of that if you want," Lieutenant Hoberman offered.

"That might be best," Roan agreed. "She wasn't too happy with us the last time we spoke."

Megan felt weary. "She's going to blame me for her husband's death."

"It's not your fault," Roan said matter-of-factly. "Her husband started this a long time ago."

"I realize that, but her life will be shattered by the news."

"A lot of lives will be," Roan agreed. "Just look at what his actions did to the McCullens."

"They'll want to find their brothers," Megan said.

"Yes, they will." Roan angled his head toward the lieutenant. "I'm going to track down Bart Dunn. If he or one of his people killed Grace and Joe Mc-Cullen, it's time they paid."

Megan followed Roan as they stepped away from her office. She would never be able to work in there again without seeing an image of Dr. Cumberland slumped in her chair with his head blown to pieces.

"Let me call our tech team and see if I can get a current address for Dunn," Hoberman said.

Roan thanked him, then phoned Maddox to relay the news of the doctor's death.

Megan stepped inside the autopsy room where Dr. Mantle stood studying the doctor before he began the autopsy.

"You were friends, weren't you?" Megan asked.

The chief ME shrugged, his expression torn. "Yes. He delivered my two girls."

"I'm so sorry," Megan said.

He stared at her for so long that Megan's pulse clamored. Did he blame her for the doctor's death?

"You were right, Megan. Damn, I didn't want to think that he'd do anything underhanded."

Megan offered him a tentative smile. "For the record, I didn't want to believe it, either."

He adjusted his glasses. "Your questions got him killed, though."

"That wasn't my intention."

He grimaced. "No, but it was theirs." His voice dropped a decibel. "Be careful, Megan. I'd hate to have you lying here next."

Megan's heart pounded at his dark tone. Was he concerned about her safety, or was that a threat?

ROAN ENDED THE call with Maddox, his chest tight as Megan reappeared in the hallway. "Maddox is going to call Brett and Ray and fill them in." A text dinged through, and he checked it.

"I've got the address for Bart Dunn. Let's go."

Megan was pale and quiet, but he didn't push her. God knows she'd been through enough the past couple of days, then to find a coworker with his head blown off in her own office? It was enough to shake anyone.

"Where does he live?"

"A ranch about fifty miles from here."

"Are you going to call ahead and see if he's there?"

"No, I want the element of surprise on my side. If he kept those babies, well, they'd be adults now. I don't want to spook them."

Night had definitely set in, the wind howling as they left Pistol Whip. The rain had slackened, but dark clouds still shrouded the moonlight, making it seem later than it was.

His tires churned over the road leading toward the Dunns' ranch, the wilderness becoming more vast and reminded Roan of his life on the res. Megan laid her head back against the seat and closed her eyes.

For a second, he thought she might fall asleep, but she kept twitching, obviously agitated. Traffic was minimal, the area growing more desolate as he approached the ranch.

The sign for the ranch hung askew and was so faded that Roan couldn't read it. He turned down the long drive, noting overgrown pastures and fields, and a barn that looked as if it was rotting. No animals were in sight, and the white clapboard house was dingy, shutters in need of repair.

"It looks like Dunn hasn't kept up his land," Megan said.

A rusty truck sat in front of the house, a beagle lying on the porch. Roan parked and they walked up to the house together. He kept one hand on his gun, alert and ready in case they were walking into an ambush.

He rapped the door knocker, slanting a look at the

dog who groaned and lifted his head, then dropped it back down as if he was too tired or old to do anything else. Footsteps shuffled inside, and the door squeaked open.

A pudgy woman with short curly brown hair answered, leaning on a cane.

"Mrs. Dunn?" Roan asked.

"Yeah, that's me."

Roan identified himself and Megan. "We'd like to talk to you and your husband."

She made a sarcastic sound. "My husband doesn't live here. He hasn't in a long time."

Roan frowned. "What about your sons?"

The woman pinned him with angry eyes. "I don't know who you think you are, but I don't have any sons."

Chapter Twenty

Megan studied the woman's reaction as she gripped the door edge. Why was she denying she had children? They could easily find that out.

"I beg your pardon," Roan said, "but I was told you had twin boys."

The woman's face turned ghostly white. "Where did you hear that?"

"From Dr. Cumberland," Megan said, the doctor's eyes haunting her.

Mrs. Dunn shook her head in denial. "You have the wrong information. I…can't help you."

She started to slam the door in their faces, but Roan caught it and shouldered his way inside.

"Stop it, you can't come in here!" Mrs. Dunn shrieked.

"I can and I'm going to," Roan said bluntly.

Sympathy for the woman tugged at Megan, but if she'd kidnapped the McCullen babies and knew about the murders, she wasn't an innocent.

"But… I haven't done anything wrong," she protested.

"Nobody said you did," Roan said, his tone indicating he didn't believe her.

Ignoring her, he strode through the foyer then into the hall and den. Mrs. Dunn chased him, and Megan followed, her gaze sweeping the walls for pictures of the family.

Of the McCullen boys—men.

But only a couple of oil landscapes and a saddle adorned the walls. No family pictures or chronicling of children as they grew up.

Roan paused in front of the stone fireplace. The furniture looked worn and old, the house was cold and seemed almost…empty.

Mrs. Dunn clung to her cane, panic tightening her face. "Please, I don't know why he told you that, but I lost my baby a long time ago. I…couldn't have children after that."

"Listen, Mrs. Dunn, cut the act," Roan said. "We know that your husband blackmailed Dr. Cumberland into stealing Grace and Joe McCullen's twin babies to give them to you."

She gasped, then staggered sideways. A moment later her face crumpled, and she sank onto the threadbare sofa with a sob. "I told Bart it was wrong…not to take them…"

Megan sucked in a sharp breath. "So you did know he kidnapped them?"

She made a strangled sound. "We were having a rough time, I was depressed. He was…drinking too much. He wanted to make me happy."

Megan and Roan exchanged looks. "Go on," Roan said.

"Losing our baby ripped us apart," she said in a muffled whisper. "I guess he thought giving me another child would fix things, make us closer." She dabbed at her eyes. "But when I heard him talking to his foreman about what he planned, I told him no. I didn't want to tear out some other woman's heart the way mine was."

"You told him to call it off?" Megan asked.

She nodded miserably. "But he said it was too late. We argued and I told him I didn't want someone else's children, that if he would do that, he wasn't the man I married. We…said awful things, and he left."

Roan let the silence stand for a heartbeat. "But he came back with the babies?" She looked up with such a desolate expression on her face that Megan did feel sorry for her.

"No. He said he'd risked everything for me, but I didn't appreciate it." She sighed. "Then he drove off and never came back."

Megan sat down beside the woman and rubbed her shoulders. "What about the twins?"

"I have no idea what he did with those babies." She wiped at her eyes. "Frankly, I told him I didn't want to know, that he should give them back to their family. I…prayed he did." She wiped at tears. "I even searched the news for mention of a kidnapping, but nothing ever came out, so I thought they must have been back with the family."

"Nothing came out because Dr. Cumberland lied to the parents and told them their babies died," Megan said.

The woman gasped, anguish streaking her face.

"When was the last time you talked to Bart?" Roan asked.

She grabbed a tissue and scrubbed her face. "He sends me a Christmas and birthday card every year. But he never says much in it."

"He never mentioned the babies or sent pictures of them?" Megan asked.

She shook her head. "No, like I said, I thought he gave them back." She turned a terrified look at Roan. "Why are you asking about all this now?"

ROAN STUDIED MRS. DUNN. The woman seemed sincere, and he certainly didn't see any signs that a man or any children had been around for a long time. "Because the father of those babies was recently murdered. We believe it was because he hired a PI to find his sons."

She blanched again, fingers frantically working at the tissue in her hand.

"Did you keep any of those cards and the envelopes with the postage on them?"

She bit down on her lip. "I kept them all. I… loved Bart, and I kept hoping he'd come back and we'd work things out. But losing the baby, then the whole thing with him talking crazy…it completely destroyed our marriage."

"Would you mind getting the cards and envelopes," Roan said gently. "It might help us track him down."

Panic flashed across her face. "If you find him, what are you going to do to him?"

Roan ground his teeth. "We just want to talk to him, Mrs. Dunn. If he took those babies, the family has a right to know where they are. Don't you agree?"

"Yes," she said in a choked whisper. "But…he meant well, and I still love him. I don't want to see him hurt."

Roan reached out and patted her hand. "I promise that if we find him, I'll do everything I can to make sure he's not hurt. Right now we just want to talk, that's all."

She hesitated, her expression anguished, but finally she inhaled a deep breath, stood and lumbered down the hall.

A minute later, the woman returned with a box filled with cards and envelopes. "The most recent ones are on top," she said, her tone worried.

"Thank you." Roan lifted the top one and studied the envelope. The address and postal stamp indicated it had come from Cheyenne.

Not too far away.

Roan gestured toward the box. "Do you mind if I take these with me?"

Mrs. Dunn looked hesitant, but finally nodded. "I would like them back. Please."

"Of course." He patted her hand again. "I'll take good care of them."

The woman escorted them to the door. As soon as they stepped outside, the wind picked up, swirling leaves around their feet as they hurried to his SUV.

"The last address was Cheyenne."

"For her sake, I hope we can keep that promise," Megan said as they drove away.

So did he. But if Dunn was behind these murders, and behind the threat against Megan, he'd do whatever necessary to bring him in.

THIRTY MILES DOWN the road, though, Roan sensed they weren't alone. Someone was following them. The bright lights of a van nearly blinded him as the vehicle closed in. A van with tinted windows.

"Hang on," he told Megan. "We've got company."

Megan darted a glance over her shoulder and winced. "He's speeding up."

Roan pressed the accelerator and rounded a curve, tires squealing, but the van raced closer.

"Dammit." Roan pressed the gas again, an oncoming car's lights flashing as the driver swerved to avoid him. The van let the other car pass, then sped up beside Roan.

Suddenly a gunshot pierced the air. Just like before.

He cursed again, then jerked the wheel to the left

to slam into the van, but it swerved toward him at the same time and knocked him into a spin.

"Hang on and get down, Megan!" He tried to maintain control, but a bullet shattered the windshield on his side, and when he ducked to avoid being hit, the van slammed into them again and his vehicle sped out of control.

They skidded, his SUV hit a boulder, bounced back, then flipped and rolled.

Megan screamed. He tried to put a hand out to keep her from hitting the dash, but the air bags exploded, pinning them against the seat. The car skidded a few more feet then careened into a ditch.

"Roan!" Megan shouted.

"I'm here."

Seconds later, the scent of gas assaulted him.

"We have to get out!" He fumbled, pushing at the air bag as he reached inside his pocket for a knife. He jerked it out and frantically ripped away the bag and his seat belt, then did the same for Megan.

The scent of gas grew stronger, then a spark ignited. God, the car was on fire. It would explode any minute.

"We have to hurry, Megan. The car's about to blow."

She frantically jerked at her door, but the impact had crushed the side in, and she couldn't open it. His was the same.

Flames darted up, visible through the back window. "Cover your head!" he shouted.

Megan dropped her head to her knees and covered it with her arms, and he shifted, then kicked at the front windshield. It took several attempts, but finally the glass cracked and shattered. He removed his jacket, wrapped it around his fist and used it to knock the remaining glass free.

He crawled through the opening first, kicking away broken shards on the hood, then reached for Megan. The flames bounced higher, smoke starting to fill the air. Heat seared his hands and face as he dragged Megan from the car.

Her ragged breathing punctuated the air as she gripped his arms. By the time they cleared the car, flames shot up along the doors and the sizzle of an impending explosion rent the air.

"Come on!" They ran for cover and collapsed against a tree just as the SUV burst into a fireball.

MEGAN CLUNG TO Roan as the flames lit the sky. The scent of burning metal and rubber filled the air, the sound of hissing flames echoing shrilly around her.

A second later and they would have died in that explosion.

"You didn't see him?" she whispered.

"No, but it was a van with tinted windows just like before. I couldn't get the license, though."

Megan fought a sob. She was not going to fall apart here. Even if they had come within a hairbreadth from burning to death, they were alive.

Roan rubbed her arms, his own breathing labored. Sweat beaded his face and droplets of blood dotted his arms. In spite of the jacket he'd wrapped around his fist, the glass shards had punctured his skin.

"You're hurt, Roan."

"No, I'm fine." He shrugged off her concern, retrieved his phone and called for help.

Megan tried to compose herself as an ambulance and fire truck arrived along with a deputy sheriff from Cheyenne.

The paramedics cleaned his arm and examined them both while the deputy snapped photos of the scene and listened while Roan explained about his investigation and what had happened.

"He shot at you?" the deputy asked.

"Yeah. I think it was the same man who shot at us before."

It was nearing midnight as the crime team arrived to process the car.

"I'll have one of my men carry you home. I'm going to try to locate Bart Dunn," the deputy said. "If he's at the address you gave me, I'll bring him in."

"We'd rather go with you tonight," Roan said. "I don't want this man to get word that we're on to him and disappear."

"Ma'am, are you sure you're all right with that?" the deputy asked.

Megan nodded. "Whoever did this has nearly

killed me three times now. If Mr. Dunn knows who did it, I want him locked up."

The deputy and Roan spoke to the crime team, then she and Roan climbed in the deputy's SUV. The deputy plugged the address into his GPS and eased onto the highway. Megan rode in back while Roan sat up front with the deputy who asked question after question about the investigation.

The gloomy weather intensified her anxiety as they neared the trailer park where they hoped Bart Dunn still lived.

The trailer park was run-down, weeds choked the tiny yards and battered kids' toys were scattered around.

"Dunn lives in the end one," Roan said.

The deputy cut his blue lights and coasted to the last trailer. An old rusted Impala sat on three wheels, obviously in need of repair and bodywork. There were no other cars in the drive.

"Doesn't look like anyone's home," the deputy said.

Still, he and Roan pulled their weapons as they crept from the deputy's SUV and inched up the graveled drive.

Megan held her breath, half hoping the man was there with answers, and praying he wasn't armed and dangerous.

ROAN CLENCHED HIS Glock in a white-knuckled grip as he climbed the rickety stairs to the trailer door.

The deputy veered right and inched around the back of the trailer, scanning the property beyond and searching for a back door in case the man was inside and tried to run.

Roan pressed his ear to the door and listened, but heard no movement inside. He leaned to the left to peek through the window, but the lights were off and he didn't see movement.

Shoulders tight, he raised his fist and knocked, his gun at the ready. The wind howled, rustling trees and sending a tin can rolling across the yard. He knocked again, but no one answered.

Braced for trouble, Roan turned the doorknob and eased open the door. The stench of rotting food, stale beer and cigarettes sucked the breath from him. He covered his mouth with his handkerchief, visually sweeping the den and kitchen, but no one was inside.

The couch was not only threadbare, but birds must have gotten inside, pecked the stuffing from the cushions and nested. The floor creaked as he crept to the hall and glanced in the one bedroom and bath. Mold grew along the wall and floor, trash was overflowing and the bed had fared like the couch.

He quickly surveyed the walls and furniture for photos, for some clue that Dunn had lived here with one or both of the twins, but the place was empty.

He checked the dresser drawers, desk, then returned to scour the kitchen for mail, bills or a paper trail that would clue him in to Bart Dunn's location.

Frustration knotted his gut. Dammit, they had to find the man. He was the key to locating the Mc-Cullen twins.

Chapter Twenty-One

Megan was still shaken as the deputy dropped them at Roan's cabin. The deputy had driven them first to her place, but Roan insisted she come home with him. He was ever the gentleman, the bodyguard, and refused to let her stay alone, so they took her car to his cabin. "You can use the shower first," he said as he combed the rooms to make sure no one was waiting inside.

Grateful they'd run by her house for an overnight bag, she ducked into the bathroom, stripped and stepped into the shower. Bruises colored her torso, arms and chest, and her ribs ached from the impact of the air bag.

The warm water felt heavenly, easing the tension from her limbs, and she washed the sweat and scent of smoke from her hair, although she couldn't erase the image of the burning vehicle from her mind.

As an ME, she'd seen the results of fire and smoke, and how it ravaged the human body. It was a painful way to go.

She rinsed off, desperately trying to obliterate

the thoughts. Too exhausted to care about dressing again, she pulled on a pair of pajamas, combed her hair and left it damp around her shoulders.

When she left the bathroom, she felt warm and cozy, yet she still shivered at the memory of the explosion.

Roan handed her a glass of wine as she entered the kitchen. He was halfway through a beer. She thanked him, well aware that he looked fierce and rugged with that leather tie holding back his hair. His eyes were dark with emotions—anger, worry… hunger.

"My turn."

She wanted to tell him she didn't care if he showered, that she wanted him to hold her and comfort her and…love her. But the scent of smoke lingered on him, a reminder of their close call with death.

Besides, if he stayed in the room she might throw herself at him, and if he rejected her, she wouldn't be able to stand it.

Tonight of all nights, she didn't want to be alone.

He disappeared, and she walked to the window and looked out. A few stars struggled to fight their way through the clouds, but the woods looked eerie, dark and filled with places predators could hide.

Shivering, she jerked the curtains closed, heard the shower water kick on, imagined Roan standing naked beneath it and her body heated with desire. Trembling with the urge to go to him and wait in his bedroom, she phoned Dr. Mantle and explained about the ambush, then left a message telling him she was staying at Roan's and for him to call her if he had any information on Dr. Cumberland's autopsy to share.

Too antsy to sit still, she headed to the den to pace, but as she passed the kitchen table where his computer was, her hip brushed a stack of papers and they fell onto the floor, scattering across the wood.

She stooped to pick them up, shoving the stack together, but one of the pages caught her eye.

A birth certificate. Roan's.

Curious, she couldn't help herself. She'd met his mother, but when she'd asked about his father, he'd clammed up and refused to discuss him.

She glanced down at the line where the father's name was listed and stared in shock.

Joe McCullen.

Her breath stalled in her chest. God... Roan was Joe's son. Which meant he was Maddox, Brett and Ray's half brother...

ROAN TOWEL-DRIED HIS hair as he stepped into the kitchen. He'd yanked on jeans and a shirt, although he hadn't buttoned it yet, but he was so damn hot he had to wait until he cooled down from the steam.

A startled gasp echoed from the kitchen, and he spotted Megan stooped down holding some papers. Others were scattered across the floor.

Her stunned gaze drifted up to his, and his gut

knotted when he realized she was holding his birth certificate.

Anger hardened his voice. "What are you doing? Snooping through my papers?"

"No." Her voice faltered. "Of course not. I accidentally knocked the file off and was picking it up."

He tossed the towel onto the kitchen chair and grabbed the papers from her. She made another surprised sound, then slowly stood.

"I'm sorry, Roan. I didn't mean to pry."

His jaw tightened. Suddenly his heart was beating ninety miles a minute. "But you did."

She reached for his arm, but he stepped back. "That was private."

Megan clamped her teeth over her lip, her expression full of regret. "I really didn't mean to," she said in a whisper. "Why didn't you tell me?"

He blinked, forcing emotions from his throat with a hard swallow. "Because it's none of your business."

"Did you tell Maddox?"

His eyes turned steely. "No, none of the McCullens know, and you'd better not tell them."

Hurt and bewilderment crossed Megan's face. "Why haven't you told them, Roan? They deserve to know."

"You're living in a fantasy world if you think anything good could come of that." He shoved the papers in the file and jammed it inside the desk, then slammed it shut with a bang.

"But they're your half brothers. You've been working this case because…it's personal to you." She hesitated, her breath rasping out. "That's why you've been so driven. Why it bothered you when Maddox made comments about his father and family."

"Maddox and Brett and Ray are not going to find out." He rammed his hand through his wet hair. "For God's sake, Megan, after what they went through with Bobby, they might think I had something to do with Joe's death."

"But that's ludicrous," Megan stammered. "You've been leading this investigation."

"And they could say that I steered it into one direction to deter suspicion from myself."

Megan shook her head in denial, her eyes filled with emotion. Anger…at him? Remorse?

"Maddox knows you, Roan. He knows you're an honorable man." She took a step toward him, her voice softening. "You lost your mother, you deserve to connect with the family you have left."

"Do you really think that the McCullens are going to accept me into their tight-knit family?" Roan's voice rose in pitch. "They didn't want to accept Bobby. They sure as hell aren't going to accept a half-breed. Especially when Joe didn't even know about me."

"Roan…don't put yourself down—"

"I'm not. I live in reality, Megan." He paced across the room, picked up his beer and chugged it, then set the bottle down with a thud. "You think prejudices don't exist anymore? You heard Mrs. Cumberland. She's not the only one who feels like that, either."

Megan shook her head again. "You don't know that the McCullens will feel that way, Roan. You have to at least give them a chance."

He strode back to her and gripped her arms, angry and hurting and wanting her so bad his damn teeth ached. "Let it go, Megan. The McCullens are not going to find out. I am going to track down the person who killed Joe and his wife. But I want nothing in return." He shook her gently. "Do you understand?"

Her eyes glittered as she stared at him, a tear sparkling on her eyelash. "Yes, Roan, I promise, your secret is safe with me."

Dammit, he released her so swiftly she stumbled backward, then he looked down at his hands. Had he been too harsh and hurt her?

He'd never forgive himself if he had.

MEGAN SENSED ROAN'S withdrawal and couldn't allow him to believe that he didn't deserve to be a McCullen.

She gingerly touched his arm. "Roan, look at me."

He stepped away in an attempt to escape her touch. But Megan moved faster than he'd anticipated and cradled his face between her hands. "Look at me," she whispered. "Don't sell yourself short. You may not have been raised a McCullen, but you're a self-made man. That's even more admirable."

He dropped his head forward, his jaw clenched. "Stop it, Megan. I don't want anything from the McCullens."

"I understand," Megan said softly. "But that still doesn't mean that you aren't as good as they are." She stood on tiptoe and brushed a kiss across his cheek. "You are strong and honest and you protect others. You sacrifice yourself to keep the people in this town safe, including the half brothers who are clueless as to how much you're sacrificing by keeping your silence."

"You can't give up something you never had," Roan said gruffly.

She brushed another kiss along his other cheek. "Yes, you can. You can miss family. You can miss having the love and support of people who are like you. And whether you realize it or not, even without Joe McCullen or his other sons knowing about you, you became an honorable decent man. A selfless man who has been fighting for justice for Joe even though you expect nothing in return."

Roan's breathing sounded choppy in the dark silence that followed. Megan's heart pounded with the need to comfort him and convince him he was worthy of love. Of the McCullen family.

At the same time her blood heated with the need to be closer to him, to feel his lips against hers. His mouth on her mouth. His hands on her body.

Her breath hitched, and his tortured gaze found hers. Something hot and passionate burst to life between them.

"Megan…"

"Don't think about it," she said in a raw whisper. "I know there are no promises, and I don't care. I just want to be with you tonight."

Roan's expression softened, although the intensity still remained, but instead of pain, hunger flared in his eyes. Emboldened by that sign, her own hunger spiraled out of control, and she pressed her lips to his.

Roan grunted, then suddenly gave in to his need and the chemistry between them, and swept her in his arms. Megan's heart raced as he carried her to his bedroom.

The room was just as masculine as Roan. Evidence of his Native American roots shone in the arrowheads and art on the walls. His bed was covered in a quilt designed with Indian symbols and a painting of a wild herd of mustangs hung above his bed.

He was like those mustangs in his raw primal energy and connection to the earth, but even with his fierce hunger for her, he possessed a tenderness that made her desire grow with every touch.

He stripped her pajamas and she pushed at his clothes. The sight of his bare chest bronzed with water droplets from the shower still clinging to his skin made her pulse pound.

He plunged his tongue inside her mouth, tasting

and exploring, and she met him thrust for thrust, each sweet kiss growing hotter until her body burned with need.

She trailed her hands across his bare torso, her breath hitching again as his muscles bunched beneath her touch.

She lowered her head and planted her lips where her hands had been, teasing him with kisses and flicks of her tongue, sweeping her lips across his nipples. Heat pooled in her belly at his guttural moan of pleasure.

She had a feeling Roan rarely took pleasure for himself, and she wanted this night to be one he would remember.

She pushed him back on the bed, raking her hands across his chest and down his body, looking her fill, then teasing his belly and trailing her fingers south until she reached his sex.

He groaned, then suddenly flipped her over and crawled on top of her. She cried out in pleasure as his mouth made a path down her neck to her breasts. Seconds later, his lips teased and tormented her nipples until they were hard and begging for more.

He drew one into his mouth and suckled her until she whimpered his name. Then he did the same to the other, his fingers traveling along her hips to her stomach and lower to tease her lips apart and taunt her with his fingers.

She wanted him inside her.

"Roan," she murmured. "I need you."

He hesitated, then lifted his head to look into her face. The flare of emotions that darkened his eyes hit her with such force that she felt the first strains of an orgasm coming.

Desperate to have him join her, she lowered her hand and closed it around his thick length.

His chest heaved as he inhaled. Once more he gave in to primal needs as he covered her hand with his. For a moment, he guided them both closer to the brink, closer to planting himself inside her.

Then he muttered a protest and pulled away.

She reached for him. "Roan, please…"

"Condom," he said in a gruff whisper.

She nodded, grateful he'd thought of it, yet hating to wait a second longer until he could be inside her.

ROAN FOUGHT THE intense need to make Megan his, but her fingers and mouth had robbed him of any rational sense. All he knew was that he couldn't walk away from her tonight.

She didn't expect more. She'd said that.

But dammit, he wanted to give her more.

Don't think, she'd told him.

With the hunger burning through his blood, how could he think?

He grabbed the condom from his nightstand, ripped the foil packet open with his teeth, rolled it on and pressed the tip of his erection against her wet center.

Megan undulated her hips, at the same time clawing at his back and pressing him closer. Skin against skin. Heat against heat.

Passion, need and a hungry desperation drove him inside her. She arched her back, raised her hips and met him thrust for thrust, her throaty cry mimicking his own male sound of pleasure as they rode the waves together.

Her body convulsed, her nails dug into his back and he closed his eyes and lost himself in the woman beneath him.

He'd never lost himself in anyone before.

The words *I love you* teetered on the edge of his tongue, but he caught himself and whispered her name again instead.

As his release claimed him, he memorized the moment to keep him company when she was gone.

MEGAN STARTLED THE next morning when her cell phone rang. She felt sore and sated and…content. In spite of the fact that they'd almost died last night, making love to Roan had made her feel more alive than she'd ever felt before.

She snuggled next to him, raking her fingers along his smooth chest, smiling as he groaned in his sleep. They had made love over and over during the night, sometimes slow and tender, at other times fast and furious as if they knew they only had one night to experience the passion.

The phone buzzed again. Damn.

Remembering they had unanswered questions

and that Bart Dunn was still missing, she grabbed her phone from the nightstand and checked the number.

Dr. Mantle.

Instantly her nerves jumped to alert.

She rolled sideways and punched Connect. "Hello."

"Megan, I finished Dr. Cumberland's autopsy last night. I need you to meet me at the morgue to discuss the results."

Megan's heart thudded. "What did you find?"

"I can't talk about it over the phone. Just come to the morgue asap."

Megan glanced over her shoulder at Roan, who was now wide-awake and watching her like a hawk.

"All right, I'll be right there."

She disconnected, then grabbed her robe and slipped it on. She had to shower before she met her boss. But Roan caught her arm.

"What was that about and where are you going?"

His possessive tone both disturbed her and awakened a tender feeling toward him. Maybe they had the possibility of more than one night.

"That was the chief ME calling about Dr. Cumberland's autopsy. He said I needed to meet him. He must have found something."

"It wasn't a suicide?"

"He wouldn't say. But, Roan, I have to go."

"You're not going anywhere without me." He slipped from bed and strode naked to the bathroom, leaving her to admire his muscular backside and wanting him all over again.

DAMMIT, ROAN WANTED Megan again. And again. And again.

Maybe he wanted her all the time.

Not a good idea.

Remembering his vehicle had died a fiery death the night before, he quickly showered so he could ride with Megan to the hospital.

No way in hell he'd allow her to go anywhere alone today. Not after last night.

Not with a killer still on the loose.

By the time he made it to the kitchen, she was dressed and ready, her hair pulled into that tight bun again. The ME back in control.

A smile curved his mouth. He could rip out that bun and ram inside her and make her lose control again.

Make her want him the way he wanted her.

He had a serious problem.

"Do you want me to drop you somewhere?" Megan asked. "Maybe to get another police car?"

"I'm going with you first, then I'll get another vehicle," he said in a tone that brooked no argument.

She retrieved her keys from her purse and they hurried to her van together.

She drove through the drive-in at the local hamburger joint and picked up coffee while he phoned to arrange another car for himself and to fill Maddox in. Maddox was sleeping, so he told Rose to have Maddox call him.

The rest of the ride to the hospital, he silently argued with himself over how and when to end this thing with Megan.

Because it had to end.

They'd had wild, crazy, erotic sex because they'd almost died last night. They were high on adrenaline and fear. Nothing more.

Except maybe…he wanted it to be more.

He wanted what his brothers had.

Not the land or money or name. The love.

But all his life that had seemed as elusive as a father whose name he hadn't known.

How could he think of Maddox, Brett and Ray as brothers when he'd lived all his life as a loner? When they wouldn't ever consider him a real brother.

Megan parked, and they walked up to the building in silence. Was she having regrets about sleeping with him?

Dawn cracked the sky as they entered. The elevator ride was short, and the halls seemed empty and dark. The hair on the back of his neck stood on end as she used her key card to enter the morgue. Déjà vu struck him. The last time they'd come here they'd found Dr. Cumberland dead. Blood everywhere.

The doors swished open, and he hesitated to search the hall before they went into the autopsy area, but Megan suddenly made a strangled sound.

He jerked his head toward her, at the same time reaching for his weapon. It was too late.

Dr. Mantle was nowhere to be seen. Instead, a white-haired, craggy-faced man grabbed Megan around the neck and pointed a gun at her head.

Chapter Twenty-Two

Roan barely controlled his rage at seeing the man's arm tighten around Megan's throat. She coughed, gasping for air, but he dragged her in front of him, shielding himself with her body.

Coward.

Roan pulled his Glock and aimed it at the man. "Let me guess, you must be Bart Dunn."

"You should have left things alone like I told you to." He cocked the gun at Megan's temple, and her eyes widened in terror. "Now drop it or I shoot her in the head."

"Just like you did Dr. Cumberland," Roan said through clenched teeth.

"I didn't shoot him. He was so driven by guilt he took care of that for me." His gun hand trembled, making Roan's lungs squeeze for air.

"Listen, Dunn," Roan said in a quiet tone—a struggle when he wanted to rip the man apart limb by limb. "We know what happened, all about you and Dr. Cumberland. How you killed Grace Mc-

Cullen and stole her twin babies, then the doctor covered it up."

His beady gray eyes bore into Roan's. "All that, and my wife wouldn't even take those babies," he growled. "I loved her so much. All I wanted to do was make up for losing our son."

Roan lowered his voice to a sympathetic pitch, hoping to connect with the man. "That must have been awful. I lost my mother and it damn near ripped my heart out. I can't imagine losing a child."

"We were going to name him after me," Dunn said in a voice that warbled with grief. "Little Bart. We had his crib all ready, the room painted blue, my wife decorated it with trains…but then everything went wrong."

"And you blamed Dr. Cumberland," Roan said.

Rage flared on the man's face, contorting the grief-stricken man to a bitter one. "It was his fault. My little Bart died before we even had a chance to hold him." He had a faraway look in his eyes as if he was reliving the nightmare.

"I'm sorry," Megan said in a rough whisper. "Really sorry, Mr. Dunn."

He seemed to loosen his hold on her for a second. "You can't know what it was like, seeing that tiny infant lying there. So cold. Not moving. We kept waiting on him to cry, hoping and praying, but he never did." Tears leaked from his eyes. "My wife was so devastated I thought I was going to lose her, too. She was bleeding a lot and almost died. But Dr.

Cumberland managed to save her." The gun wobbled in his hand. "It still didn't make up for little Bart being gone."

"Nothing could," Megan said softly.

"So you told the doctor to get you another baby," Roan said, filling in the blanks. "Did Morty Burns and his wife, Edith, help you? Were they in on it?"

"No, but later Morty had heard me and my wife aruging and figured it out. He wanted money to keep quiet," Dunn spit out. "I paid them at first, but it got to be too much."

"So you killed them," Megan whispered. "And you pushed me into the street and later attacked me in the morgue."

"But you kept asking questions."

Roan gritted his teeth. "All those people dead—Grace, Joe, the PI? You murdered them all to keep them from finding those twins."

Dunn wiped sweat from his neck. "I couldn't go to jail, not when I'd already lost so much."

"How did you poison Joe?" Megan asked.

The man huffed. "It wasn't that hard. Even when he was sick, Joe insisted on his nightly scotch. I had a bottle sent to him as a gift from the Cattlemen's club. He never tasted a thing."

"Dr. Cumberland kidnapped the McCullen babies and told Grace they died?" Roan asked.

"He didn't want to, but he messed up that day with us and I told him I'd ruin his reputation. After all, he destroyed my life."

Roan inched toward him. "Now the truth has come out, Dunn. We talked to your wife."

Pain wrenched his face. "She told me to take those babies back, but how could I? The deed was done. After all I sacrificed for her, she didn't want them."

"Because they belonged to another mother," Megan said. "She didn't want that woman to feel the same kind of pain she felt."

He pressed the gun at her temple again. Roan froze, terrified the man would shoot.

He couldn't lose Megan.

"You did what you could for your wife," Roan said, hoping to assuage the man's pride. "But killing Dr. Lail is not right and you know it. Nobody can bring your son back, but she had nothing to do with your loss. Don't let anyone else die. If your son had lived, he wouldn't want that."

An anguished sob escaped the man, but instead of releasing Megan, he dragged her backward. "I'm not going to jail," he said bitterly. "I'll release her once I get away."

Megan gave Roan a brave look, but Roan had a bad feeling that if he didn't save Megan now, the man would shoot her before he disappeared.

One more step and Dunn was near the rear door. Roan gave Megan a signal to drop, and she elbowed Dunn and ducked as Roan charged the man with his weapon.

"Drop it!" Roan shouted to Dunn.

Dunn fired. Megan screamed and rolled out of the way. Roan vaulted toward Dunn, but he fired again. This time the bullet pierced Roan's chest.

Roan fired a round from his own gun, and Dunn's body bounced against the wall, blood spurting from his chest. Dunn dropped his gun to the floor, his look startled as he fell to his knees, then collapsed.

Roan struggled to remain on his feet, but blood oozed from his wound and he staggered sideways. He managed to kick Dunn's gun out of the bastard's reach before he went down on his knees.

"Roan!" Megan scrambled to help him, and he slumped against her.

Roan still kept his gun trained on Dunn. "Where are the McCullen twins?"

Dunn looked up at him with dazed eyes, then coughed blood. "I...couldn't get caught..."

Roan jammed the gun at the man's forehead, praying he hadn't hurt those babies. "What did you do with them?"

"I left them at a church," he rasped.

"Where are they now?"

He coughed, spitting blood. "Don't...know."

"What was the name of the church?"

Dunn gagged for a breath.

Roan shook him. "Tell me the name of the church."

But Dunn's eyes rolled back in his head, and his chest jerked with his last breath.

Dammit. Roan reached for Megan to keep from passing out, but lost the battle.

MEGAN SWIPED AT tears as she eased Roan to the floor. The gunshot looked…bad.

She called the ER for help while she grabbed some cloths, folded them up and pressed them against Roan's wound to stem the blood flow. Terrified Roan would die, she sank to the floor and cradled his head in her lap while she waited on the medics.

"Please don't die on me," she whispered. "I love you, Roan. You're the only man I've ever felt this way about."

Tears blurred her vision, but she blinked them away. She had to be strong. Should call someone.

Maddox. Brett. Ray. Roan's half brothers.

A helpless feeling overcame her. She would let Maddox know Roan had been shot, but she couldn't tell them the truth about his paternity. She'd promised Roan.

"Dr. Lail?" A voice shouted to her from the cold room, and she frowned.

"I'll be right back, Roan. Help is on its way."

She gently laid Roan's head back on a pad, then hurried to the cold room.

"Megan! Get me out of here!"

"Dr. Mantle!"

"Some bastard made me call you and locked me in here," he yelled.

"So there was nothing odd about Cumberland's autopsy?" Megan asked.

"Just that he shot himself."

She hurried to retrieve her keys, then unlocked the door. Dr. Mantle appeared to be unharmed, but he was steaming mad. "Is that crazy man still here?"

"He's dead," Megan said as she led him back to Roan. "He shot the deputy sheriff, too."

His shocked gaze flew to hers. "What the hell?"

She stooped to check Roan's pulse while she explained to her boss what they'd learned about Dr. Cumberland.

Seconds later, footsteps pounded, and the ER team raced in. They checked Roan's vitals, then hoisted him onto a gurney and rushed toward the elevator.

Megan followed, her heart in her throat. Roan couldn't die and leave her. She needed him.

THREE HOURS LATER and Megan thought she was going to go insane. Roan's prognosis wasn't good, but he was in surgery.

What in the world was taking so long?

She'd paid Maddox a quick visit to inform him about what had happened. He was supposed to be released, but insisted on joining her in the waiting room. Rose and Mama Mary both showed up to hold vigil, as well. So had Brett and Ray.

"Dunn didn't say what happened to the twins?" Maddox asked.

Megan shook her head. "I'm sorry. He said his wife told him to take them back. He was afraid of being caught so he dropped them at a church."

Brett cleared his throat. "What church?"

Megan knotted her hands together. "He died before he could tell us."

Ray cursed, and Megan's heart went out to the three men. They wanted to find their missing brothers.

Yet they had no idea that the man who'd found their parents' killer and discovered they had twin brothers was also their blood kin.

It wasn't fair to Roan.

She paced to the nurses' station again. "Have you heard anything from the doctor about Deputy Whitefeather's surgery?"

The nurse's brow furrowed. "He's coming out to talk to you in a minute."

Megan thanked her and strode over to the door of the waiting room to keep watch.

Seconds dragged into excruciating minutes. When the surgeon finally appeared, his grave expression made her stomach revolt.

"What's wrong?"

"I'm afraid he's not doing too well. We got the bullet out, but it punctured his heart, and he was bleeding internally. He needs a transfusion, but we're short on his blood type. He also has a rare genetic marker."

The doctor ran a hand over his surgical cap.

"Does he have family? Someone who could possibly donate blood for a transfusion. Even then, it may be touch and go for a while."

Fear clawed at Megan. She'd vowed to keep quiet about Roan's paternity, but how could she keep that promise if his life depended on his half brothers?

There really was no other choice.

"Let me talk to the McCullens and I'll get back to you."

He nodded. "We're asking around other hospitals to try to locate a blood match."

Megan thanked him, took a deep breath and hurried to talk to Maddox and his brothers.

"How is he?" Maddox asked.

"He lost a lot of blood and needs a transfusion." She explained about his blood type and that a family member would be the best bet.

"Does he have family?" Brett asked.

"He never mentioned any to me," Maddox said. "He lost his mother a few months ago."

Megan wet her parched lips with her tongue. "Actually, he does have some family."

"Who?" Ray asked.

Brett gestured toward his phone. "I'll call them."

"That's just it," Megan said. "It's not that simple."

Mama Mary gave Megan a sympathetic look. "What is it, honey?"

Megan sighed, prayed the McCullens wouldn't balk at what she had to say, then began to explain.

Maddox sat with his head down, shaking it back

and forth in denial. Brett looked shell-shocked while Ray's dark look reeked of suspicion.

"Why didn't he tell us?" Ray asked.

"He didn't know until his mother died and he found his birth certificate. She met your father long before he married your mother. Apparently when she got pregnant, she never told Joe. I guess with the cultural differences, she didn't want to cause trouble."

"But Roan has known for months and works for me," Maddox said. "How could he keep this from us?"

Megan crossed her arms. "He didn't know how you would react. He was afraid you'd accuse him of wanting something from you like Bobby did."

Brett winced. "What *does* he want?"

"Nothing," Megan said, a trace of anger in her voice. "That's the point. He didn't want anything from you, but when he discovered your father—his father—was murdered, he did everything possible to find his killer."

A tense silence ensued. Mama Mary clapped her hands. "He's a good man, boys. He figured out Ms. Grace was murdered and that her babies might still be alive."

"That's right," Megan said. "And he was shot and almost died searching for the answers for you."

Another silence, then Maddox gripped the edge of his wheelchair. "I'm going to get tested to see if my blood will work."

Brett nodded. "I'm right behind you."

Ray followed. "Me, too."

Mama Mary hugged each of them as they filed out to see if they could help save Roan.

Chapter Twenty-Three

Megan waited with Mama Mary and Rose while Maddox, Brett and Ray had blood drawn. Brett and Ray must have called their wives because Willow and Scarlet both showed up. Mama Mary introduced them to Megan, then took Brett's little boy to the cafeteria for ice cream.

The older woman was far more than a cook and housekeeper—she was a mother to them all and the glue that held the McCullens together.

Maddox and Brett returned a few minutes later without Ray. Their faces looked strained, the night's revelations still sinking in.

"Ray is a match," Maddox said.

"Thank God." Megan couldn't hide her relief. Both Maddox and Brett looked at her with narrowed eyes, but their wives squeezed her arm as if they completely understood.

The next few hours dragged by excruciatingly slowly. Ray did the transfusion, but still they waited to see how Roan would respond.

Meanwhile, Ray made some calls and learned

that Elmore Clark had nothing to do with the trouble at Horseshoe Creek. Apparently he'd left town a couple of years ago and settled in with his daughter and her children.

Since only family was allowed, each of the men had taken a turn visiting Roan.

But Megan wanted to be with him. She needed to touch him, to feel that he was still alive, to see his chest rising with each breath and the color returning to his complexion.

It *would* return. He *would* be all right. She couldn't allow herself to think otherwise.

Mama Mary drove Brett's little boy home, and the McCullen men insisted their wives go with her. They were possessive, protective and three cowboys who adored the women they'd married.

Megan wanted that with Roan.

But what would he want when he woke up?

ROAN REACHED FOR his mother's outstretched hand. "I've missed you, son."

Washed out sunlight cast shadows around her angelic form, but he recognized her face. Her sweet smile. Her long, dark braid.

Chants in his Native American language echoed from somewhere in the distance, maybe behind the moon. The shaman stood over him, his feathers swaying as he waved his arms and hands above Roan, performing one of the sacred songs that their people sang when someone passed.

He was dead.

His mother…the light…the music…

Darkness swallowed him, and he was spinning and falling, clawing the emptiness for his mother's hand, for the light, but his hand connected with air and the light faded.

Was he headed into Hell?

The sound of another voice cut into his confusion, soothing his fears. "Roan, you're going to be all right."

He struggled to open his eyes, but his lids felt heavy and he hurt all over. Pain burned through his veins and his skin felt like it was on fire.

He was in Hell.

"Come back to me, Roan, please, I need you."

That sweet voice…if he was dead and in Hell, so was she. But that wasn't right. Megan was too kind and honorable, too good to land in the fiery depths below the ground.

"I'm right here, and so are Maddox and Brett and Ray. They're outside in the waiting room."

Waiting room?

He wasn't in Hell, after all. It just felt like it.

An image of Megan crawling on top of him, naked and so beautiful he could hardly breathe for wanting her, floated to him, wrapping him in the seductiveness of her voice.

Her gentle hands brushed his cheek, and then

her lips touched his, and he floated off, dreaming he was in Heaven.

Some time later, hours or days, he had no idea, pain wrenched him from his peaceful sleep. He stirred with a moan and reached for the image of Megan naked and loving him. It was the only comfort he'd known.

But when he opened his eyes, Maddox stood beside his bed, looking serious and worried and… angry.

Roan blinked, squinting through the fog of drugs and the haze of his muddled mind, then saw Brett and Ray beside him. Arms crossed. Frowning faces. Suspicious eyes.

They didn't have to say a word. Somehow they knew the truth about who he was.

A sense of betrayal cut through him like a knife. The only person who could have told them was Megan.

And she'd promised to keep his secret.

But she had lied.

MEGAN THANKED THE nurse for updating her on Roan's condition. She'd also been kind enough to sneak Megan in for a visit during the long, dark hours of the night. Only after she'd seen that Roan was indeed breathing did Megan allow herself to doze in the waiting room.

Morning coffee in hand, she stepped to the edge

of the room and saw the three McCullen men standing by his bed.

"You should have told me," Maddox said. "I would have understood."

Roan wheezed a breath. He still looked pale, and wires and tubes were strung from him to machines that beeped and got on her nerves, but at least he was alive. "You had enough trouble on your plate," he said gruffly. "Besides, I don't want or expect anything from you. You owe me nothing."

He said it with such conviction that Megan's heart ached for him. Roan had gotten the raw end of the deal, but unlike Bobby, who'd allowed his bitterness and self-pity to turn him into a vindictive person, Roan had thrived and made a man of himself.

"You found the man who killed our father," Brett said, his voice thick with emotions.

"And our mother." Ray pinched the bridge of his nose. "You don't know what that means to us."

Maddox cleared his throat. "We would have never known the truth," he said. "Or that we have two more brothers."

"That is, if they're still alive," Brett muttered.

"Dunn said he left them at a church," Roan said. "That's a place to start."

The three McCullens nodded, then one by one shook Roan's hand. Megan blinked back tears at the scene.

Maybe Roan had been wrong about them accepting him. For his sake, she hoped so.

"We should let you get some rest," Maddox said.

The other two agreed, and they assured Roan they'd be back.

"Thanks for the transfusion," Roan said to Ray. "You saved my life."

Ray gripped Roan's hand. "That's what brothers do." He angled his head toward the door. "You can thank Megan, too. I think she wants to see you."

The three men left together, and Megan crossed the room, but the smile faded from Roan's face. Instead a bitter scowl darkened his eyes.

"You made a promise and you broke it."

The coldness in his tone cut Megan to the bone. "I'm sorry, but you were dying, Roan. I had to do something."

"It doesn't matter. I trusted you and you betrayed me." His Adam's apple bobbed as he swallowed. "Leave me alone."

Megan reached for his hand to tell him how much she loved him, but he closed his eyes and turned away from her, shutting her out as if he was cutting her out of his life.

ROAN DIDN'T KNOW what to say to the McCullens. He'd been alone so long that he was far more comfortable by himself than having other people in his life.

And Megan…

She'd only been gone a few hours now and he missed her. His dreams after she'd left had been mixed with visions of them making love and with her walking down the aisle with another man.

Then there were horrible nightmares about Megan being murdered, of finding her in one of the drawers at the morgue.

Of losing her forever.

He'd woken in a cold sweat with tears streaming down his face.

He couldn't survive loving Megan and having something bad happen to her.

Besides, he had nothing to offer her.

It was better to break it off before anyone got hurt.

HURT SWELLED INSIDE MEGAN.

It had been three days since Roan's surgery. He was improving, and the doctors expected him to make a full recovery. The McCullen men and Mama Mary had visited him daily. Mama Mary seemed to have had already adopted him as another son and had snuck him homemade soup and some of her huckleberry pie.

Megan's heart twisted. She was glad the family had accepted him.

But Roan refused to see her.

Was he simply angry that she'd told the McCullens about his relationship to them? Or…did he really not care about her?

Had he only taken her to bed because they'd been thrown together and in danger and she was… available?

Self-doubts assailed her as she finished an autopsy on a man who'd had a seizure while driving and ended up wrapping his car around a tree.

Determined to reach Roan, she washed her hands, removed her lab coat and headed to the second floor where he was recovering. When she reached his room, he was trying to get out of bed and arguing with one of the nurses.

"Tell the doctor I'm ready to go home. I'm not a damn invalid."

Megan laughed at his obstinate tone. He was definitely feeling better.

Still, he winced as the nurse helped him back to bed, a sign he had a long way to go before he was back to normal.

Her stomach fluttered with nerves as she stepped aside to allow the nurse to exit the room. When she walked in, she was so anxious to see him that his scowl didn't faze her.

"Hi, Roan."

A muscle ticked in his jaw. "What are you doing here? The case is over."

His look indicated they were also over.

She inhaled a deep breath and stepped closer to his bed. "I know that. But I miss you."

Some emotion she didn't understand flickered in his eyes. "Megan, don't."

"Don't what? Don't be honest?" she said softly. "Don't care about you?"

"Don't make something out of what happened between us. It was just one night of sex. Nothing more."

She'd been afraid he felt that way, but hearing the words felt as if he'd stabbed her in her heart.

"But—"

"There is no but." He jerked the sheet up over himself, but the movement only caused her to notice his bare legs poking out from that hospital gown.

God, she wanted to crawl in bed beside him, run her foot up his calf, her hands over his chest. She wanted to love him and for him to love her back.

All the things her father said to her growing up rose to the surface. She had her brains, her job. Hell, she was married to her job.

No man would ever marry her because she wasn't the pretty girl they wanted on their arm.

"I understand," she said, grateful her voice didn't break. "I won't bother you again." Terrified, she might break down in front of him, she turned and ran from the room.

She made it all the way to the elevator before she burst into tears.

She swiped angrily at them as the elevator doors opened and out stepped Mama Mary.

Embarrassed, she forced a smile, but her tears must have given her away.

"What's wrong, dear? Is it Mr. Roan? Did something happen?"

She shook her head. "He's all right. It's just...he doesn't want me."

Mama Mary gaped at her, then folded her in her arms. "Come on, honey, and tell me all about it."

Megan had stood alone for so long that she welcomed the woman's motherly embrace and allowed her to usher her to the cafeteria for coffee and a good cry.

ROAN WAS TIRED of the hospital, tired of the nurses hovering, tired of feeling weak and damn near helpless.

He wanted to go home and sulk by himself in his own place.

Except Megan had been there with him, leaving her sweet feminine scent on his sheets, and images of her climbing on top of him and tormenting him with her body in his mind.

How could he sleep in his own bed now without remembering that night?

You told her it meant nothing.

This time he'd lied.

It had meant everything.

He squeezed his eyes closed, desperately trying to blot the memory, but he could see her head thrown back, her breasts swaying above him, her lips parted and closing around his sex.

Dammit…

Mama Mary knocked, then lumbered in. "Mr. Roan, I hear you've been giving everyone here fits."

In just a few short days, he'd come to love the older woman. He especially loved her pies.

Did she have one with her today?

No…her hands were empty. And for the first time since she'd taken it upon herself to cheer him up daily, she wasn't smiling.

"I'm ready to go home."

"Yeah. You also made Ms. Megan cry." She huffed and planted her hands on her ample hips. "And that girl seems like a tough one. Not like a crier."

She *was* tough. "She was crying?"

Mama Mary marched over to him. "If you don't love her, I get that, but that girl was plumb devastated with worry the night she brought you in. She waited here all night praying and frettin'. She's crazy in love with you, Mr. Roan."

Roan clenched the sheets in a white-knuckled grip. He didn't know how to respond. Megan had never said she loved him.

Because you didn't give her the chance.

"Worst thing is, she thinks you don't want her 'cause she's not one of those beauty queen types."

That took him by surprise. "What?"

In spite of the fact that he was bandaged, she

actually poked him in the chest. "You heard me. Seems her daddy did a number on her. Told her she wasn't pretty like her sister, that girls like her had to use their brains to get by." She made an indignant sound. "Now, I sure as heck agree with that. But Ms. Megan is strong and brave, and she cares about folks with all her heart, and that makes her ten times more beautiful than any of those plastic model types with their fancy clothes and three-inch heels and gobs of makeup."

Roan remembered the way she'd looked with her hair tumbling around her shoulders, with her eyes dark with passion. Then her comment about being a cactus. "I agree."

Mama Mary narrowed her eyes. "You do?"

"Yes, of course. She's the most beautiful woman I've ever met."

She stared at him with a confused look. "But you don't have feelings for her?"

Roan looked away. Mama Mary was way too perceptive. "I didn't say that. I just don't have anything to offer her."

"What kind of foolishness are you talking about?" She tsked at him. "All a woman really wants is a man to love her." She poked him again. "*Do* you love her?"

Roan chewed the inside of his cheek. "It's not that simple."

"It is if you want it to be. If you love her, get up out of that bed and tell her."

Roan looked at the door, then at Mama Mary, and an image of Megan crying taunted him. She thought he didn't love her because she wasn't beautiful enough.

He wasn't accustomed to being part of a family, to having brothers, or a mother figure, to…having someone love him.

But hadn't he envied Maddox and Rose?

He had wanted what they had. Maybe he had it with Megan.

But he'd been too stubborn and cowardly to admit his feelings. Too afraid of losing her and being hurt.

In protecting himself, he'd hurt her. The one person who loved him for himself.

He shoved at the covers. "Push that wheelchair over here. I'm going to see her now."

"Hot damn." Mama Mary gave him a big hug that nearly tore out his stitches, but he chuckled as she pulled away and pushed him into the chair. He wheeled himself to the elevator and started toward the morgue, but decided to stop at the flower shop instead.

Fear pressed against his heart as he made his purchase and rode the elevator to the morgue. What if he'd hurt her so badly that she couldn't forgive him?

Chapter Twenty-Four

Megan splashed cold water on her face and patted her tear-swollen eyes dry.

Good grief, she couldn't believe she'd poured out her heart and soul to Mama Mary. But that woman had a way of wrapping her arms around you that made you feel like you'd come home.

Maddox, Brett and Ray had missed growing up with their birth mother, but they'd been blessed by having a wonderful woman like Mama Mary in their lives.

Roan would be blessed with that now, too. She could already hear the affection in the woman's voice when she said his name. One of the nurses had told her that Mama Mary had been doting on him and spoiling him rotten.

Roan deserved it.

She blew her nose, then gave herself a pep talk before returning to work. She was fine. She might be alone, but she had her job.

Yep, all those dead people waiting on her. But dead people didn't talk to you or hold you at night and keep you warm when your nightmares crept up on you.

Maybe she'd get a dog. Or a cat. She could become one of those cat collectors who had half a dozen…

She tossed the paper towel in the trash, dabbed a little powder on her cheeks, then stepped from the bathroom and headed back to the morgue. When she arrived, she was surprised to see Roan in a wheelchair.

"What are you doing here?" She skimmed her gaze over his torso. His bandage was still in place, but his coloring was better.

"I came to see you." His jaw tightened as if he might have come under duress. "You've been crying."

Compassion softened the accusation, and a blush heated her neck. She didn't intend to tell him about her meltdown. "What do you want, Roan?"

Her voice sounded harsher than she'd intended, but he had dismissed her earlier as if she was nothing. Better he think she was angry than hurt.

"I'm sorry for hurting you," he said, his voice hoarse.

So much for hiding her feelings.

"You were just being honest, Roan. I'm a big girl. I'm fine."

"Well, I'm not fine."

Worry knifed through her. "What's wrong? Are you in pain? Are your stitches coming loose?"

He pushed himself to stand and pulled a bouquet of sunflowers from behind his back. "This is not about my gunshot wound." He took a step closer to her, and Megan's chest squeezed.

"Roan, you shouldn't be down here. You need to go back to your room and rest."

"I can't rest until I make things right."

Her heart fluttered, but she ordered herself not to latch on to hope.

"What do you mean?"

"I mean you're not a cactus, you're a sunflower." He thrust them in her hand. "And I was a coward," he said bluntly. "I lied to you before."

She smiled at the sunflowers in her hand. Was he saying what she thought he was saying? "Lied about what?"

"About that night meaning nothing. It was…" He cradled her hand in his and pressed it over his heart. "It was everything to me. *You* are everything to me."

Megan's heart pounded. "I am?"

"Yes." A smile curved his sensual mouth. "It hurt so much when I lost my mother that I vowed never to love anyone ever again. I…didn't think I could stand that kind of pain."

Megan's heart fluttered.

"Then I found you and my brothers and I didn't think I deserved any of you."

"Oh, Roan, that's not true. You are the most honorable man I've ever met."

He lifted her hand and kissed her fingers. "And you are the most beautiful woman I've ever met."

"Roan, you don't have to stay that. It's not true—"

"It is true." He stroked her arms with his hands. "Your father was wrong to make you think that you aren't beautiful."

Her breath caught. "My God, Mama Mary told you."

He nodded, but his eyes didn't hold pity. They held a tenderness that made her heart fill with warmth.

"I love you, Megan. I...don't want to lose you." He leaned closer and brushed a kiss across her lips. "I have three brothers now. I'm just getting used to that. But I still need you." He kissed her again. "I still want you."

"I want you, too," she said breathlessly.

"I love you," he whispered.

"I love you, too."

His kiss came hard and fierce this time, a give-and-take, a dance of love and promises.

When he finally pulled apart, they were both panting. "You really do need to get back to bed," she whispered.

"Not until you promise me something."

The fact that she'd broken her other promise echoed in her mind. "What? Anything..."

A teasing smile flickered in his eyes. "Promise me that you'll marry me."

Megan's heart soared with love and happiness.

She threw her arms around him and they both fell into the wheelchair, the sunflowers fluttering to the floor as she kissed him and told him yes.

Epilogue

Three weeks later

Megan smiled as Mama Mary adjusted her veil. She was marrying Roan today. The McCullen wives had welcomed her like a sister into their family and helped her put together the wedding, which was taking place at Horseshoe Creek.

Rose had found a wedding gown through her antiques shop, Vintage Treasures, that reminded Megan of the dress her mother had worn. In the dress, she felt…beautiful.

Willow and Scarlet had helped decorate the gazebo by the pond on the property that the McCullens had given Roan as a thank-you gift and a wedding present. But it meant more than a piece of land—it meant they accepted Roan as part of the McCullens.

A knock sounded at the door of the cabin where she and Roan were living temporarily until their house was built. Mama Mary answered, then returned a moment later.

"Megan, there's someone here to see you."

Megan finished applying lip gloss. "Who is it?"

"It's me, your father."

The deep baritone voice made Megan swirl around. She stared at her father, speechless for a moment. He looked older, his hair was graying and he wore a dark suit, but he still stood tall and imposing.

Mama Mary and the McCullen women slipped quietly out the door.

Her heart fluttered with dread. "Hello, Dad. What are you doing here?" Had he come to try to talk her out of marrying Roan?

"I heard you were getting married."

She nodded, braced for an argument. "I am. To Deputy Roan Whitefeather. He's a wonderful man."

Her father studied her for a second, his face twisting with emotions. "I tried to reach you several times lately, but you didn't return my calls."

"I was busy. Working."

"I know. I read about you and this deputy and what you did." His voice thickened. "I came to say I'm proud of you, Megan. I…know it's late in coming, but I'm so proud."

Tears clogged Megan's throat.

"I was…not always the most understanding father, or at least it didn't come out that way. I didn't handle losing your sister and your mother well at all, and I guess I retreated into some kind of shell."

"We were both grieving, Dad," Megan said softly.

"Yes, but I pushed you away, I let you down."

"I understood. I wasn't pretty like Shelly or Mom, not the girly girl—"

"That's just it, you are so beautiful, Megan, but in a different way. You're strong and smart and kind-hearted and…you always seemed so independent. I suppose I doted on Shelly because she was easy, and she didn't have the brains and drive you did. I thought she needed me more."

"Oh, Dad, I needed you, too." Megan swallowed, battling more tears.

"I realize that now." Her father rubbed a hand across his forehead. "Anyway, I've thought a lot about it and I want us to see each other again, to be…to build a relationship."

Megan bit down on her lip. "I'm not leaving the ME's office, Dad."

"I know that." A smile graced his mouth. "And I'm not asking you to. All I'm asking is that you give me a chance to be your father again. To have a place in your life."

How could she say no to that?

He removed a velvet box from his pocket and held it out to her. "Here, sweetheart, please open this."

Her hand trembled as she accepted the box and lifted the top. Her breath caught at the diamond earrings sparkling back. They were stunning.

"Those were your mother's. She wore them at our wedding." His tone grew gruffer. "I thought you might want to wear them today."

Tears filled Megan's eyes and she stood and

rushed to her father. "Thank you, Dad. I don't know what to say."

"Just know that she loved you, honey. I wish she was here to see you now."

"I wish she was, too," Megan said through her tears.

He closed his arms around her. "I love you, Megan. I really do. I'm sorry for wasting so much time."

"I love you, too." She kissed his cheek, then took his hand and squeezed it. "Will you walk me down the aisle?"

His gaze met hers, the pain and turmoil of their past fading away. "I would be honored."

ROAN ADJUSTED HIS bolo tie, smiling at his half brothers who'd joked about how uncomfortable they all felt in a suit. They'd been grateful he'd asked them to wear jeans and a Western duster instead.

He'd been moved when Maddox, Brett and Ray had given him the land their father had bought from Clark. They assured him he'd earned it, and they wanted him to be part of Horseshoe Creek.

His half brothers filed out from the cabin and they took their places at the gazebo the womenfolk had decorated in front of the pond on what was now his land.

Tears clouded his eyes as Megan walked across the field on her father's arm. Mama Mary had told him that the senior Dr. Lail had shown up, and he'd been nervous that Megan would be upset.

But her radiant smile as she looked up at him and then her father told him they'd made peace.

His wife-to-be looked stunning in an antique ivory lace dress. A shoulder-length veil was held in place by pearl combs, and today she'd worn her hair down, long and flowing and blowing in the wind.

He stepped up to take her hand, and she kissed him before the ceremony even started.

Laughter erupted from the McCullens and Mama Mary, and Brett's little boy clapped. Dr. Lail gave him a serious look, then shook his hand.

"Take care of my girl, she's special," he said in a gruff voice.

Roan nodded. "Yes she is, sir."

Megan kissed him again, and Roan laughed and drew her in his arms. The kiss was just a prelude of the life they were starting together.

And one day they would have a family of their own.

But today Megan was all he needed. Although he was grateful for the McCullens and the land he and Megan could now call home.

* * * * *

*Find out what really happened to
the missing McCullen twins when*
THE HEROES OF HORSESHOE CREEK
*continues later this year! Look for them
wherever Harlequin Intrigue books are sold!*

LARGER-PRINT
BOOKS!

HARLEQUIN

Presents®

GET 2 FREE LARGER-PRINT
NOVELS PLUS 2 FREE GIFTS!

YES! Please send me 2 FREE LARGER-PRINT Harlequin Presents® novels and my 2 FREE gifts (gifts are worth about $10). After receiving them, if I don't wish to receive any more books, I can return the shipping statement marked "cancel." If I don't cancel, I will receive 6 brand-new novels every month and be billed just $5.30 per book in the U.S. or $5.74 per book in Canada. That's a saving of at least 12% off the cover price! It's quite a bargain! Shipping and handling is just 50¢ per book in the U.S. and 75¢ per book in Canada.* I understand that accepting the 2 free books and gifts places me under no obligation to buy anything. I can always return a shipment and cancel at any time. Even if I never buy another book, the two free books and gifts are mine to keep forever.

176/376 HDN GHVY

Name	(PLEASE PRINT)

Address	Apt. #

City	State/Prov.	Zip/Postal Code

Signature (if under 18, a parent or guardian must sign)

Mail to the **Reader Service:**
IN U.S.A.: P.O. Box 1867, Buffalo, NY 14240-1867
IN CANADA: P.O. Box 609, Fort Erie, Ontario L2A 5X3

Are you a subscriber to Harlequin Presents® books
and want to receive the larger-print edition?
Call 1-800-873-8635 today or visit us at www.ReaderService.com.

* Terms and prices subject to change without notice. Prices do not include applicable taxes. Sales tax applicable in N.Y. Canadian residents will be charged applicable taxes. Offer not valid in Quebec. This offer is limited to one order per household. Not valid for current subscribers to Harlequin Presents Larger-Print books. All orders subject to credit approval. Credit or debit balances in a customer's account(s) may be offset by any other outstanding balance owed by or to the customer. Please allow 4 to 6 weeks for delivery. Offer available while quantities last.

Your Privacy—The Reader Service is committed to protecting your privacy. Our Privacy Policy is available online at www.ReaderService.com or upon request from the Reader Service.

We make a portion of our mailing list available to reputable third parties that offer products we believe may interest you. If you prefer that we not exchange your name with third parties, or if you wish to clarify or modify your communication preferences, please visit us at www.ReaderService.com/consumerchoice or write to us at Reader Service Preference Service, P.O. Box 9062, Buffalo, NY 14240-9062. Include your complete name and address.

LARGER-PRINT BOOKS!
GET 2 FREE LARGER-PRINT NOVELS PLUS
2 FREE GIFTS!

HARLEQUIN®

Romance

From the Heart, For the Heart

YES! Please send me 2 FREE LARGER-PRINT Harlequin® Romance novels and my 2 FREE gifts (gifts are worth about $10). After receiving them, if I don't wish to receive any more books, I can return the shipping statement marked "cancel." If I don't cancel, I will receive 4 brand-new novels every month and be billed just $5.09 per book in the U.S. or $5.49 per book in Canada. That's a savings of at least 15% off the cover price! It's quite a bargain! Shipping and handling is just 50¢ per book in the U.S. and 75¢ per book in Canada.* I understand that accepting the 2 free books and gifts places me under no obligation to buy anything. I can always return a shipment and cancel at any time. Even if I never buy another book, the two free books and gifts are mine to keep forever.

119/319 HDN GHWC

Name	(PLEASE PRINT)

Address	Apt. #

City	State/Prov.	Zip/Postal Code

Signature (if under 18, a parent or guardian must sign)

Mail to the **Reader Service:**
IN U.S.A.: P.O. Box 1867, Buffalo, NY 14240-1867
IN CANADA: P.O. Box 609, Fort Erie, Ontario L2A 5X3
Want to try two free books from another line?
Call 1-800-873-8635 or visit www.ReaderService.com.

* Terms and prices subject to change without notice. Prices do not include applicable taxes. Sales tax applicable in N.Y. Canadian residents will be charged applicable taxes. Offer not valid in Quebec. This offer is limited to one order per household. Not valid for current subscribers to Harlequin Romance Larger-Print books. All orders subject to credit approval. Credit or debit balances in a customer's account(s) may be offset by any other outstanding balance owed by or to the customer. Please allow 4 to 6 weeks for delivery. Offer available while quantities last.

Your Privacy—The Reader Service is committed to protecting your privacy. Our Privacy Policy is available online at www.ReaderService.com or upon request from the Reader Service.

We make a portion of our mailing list available to reputable third parties that offer products we believe may interest you. If you prefer that we not exchange your name with third parties, or if you wish to clarify or modify your communication preferences, please visit us at www.ReaderService.com/consumerschoice or write to us at Reader Service Preference Service, P.O. Box 9062, Buffalo, NY 14240-9062. Include your complete name and address.

HRLP15